The Magical
Matchmaker's Legacy

MORNA'S ACCOMPLICE

USA TODAY BESTSELLING AUTHOR
BETHANY CLAIRE

Editor: J.J. Archer
Cover Designed by Sarah Hansen, Okay Creations

Available in eBook, Paperback & Hardback

eBook ISBN: 978-1-947731-11-0
Paperback ISBN: 978-1-947731-12-7
Hardback ISBN: 978-1-947731-14-1

http://www.bethanyclaire.com

AUTHOR NOTE

AUTHOR NOTE: "Morna's Accomplice" is the SWEET/CLEAN version of "Love Beyond Measure," originally published in 2014 by Bethany Claire.

CHAPTER 1

Mitchell Family Estate – Lake Placid, New York—Present Day

"Pssst..."

Believing he'd heard something, but not sure enough to fully turn his head toward the sound, the corner of Cooper's right brow lifted slightly.

I grinned, making sure not to stick my head out too far past the archway. I didn't want anyone sitting in the outdoor aisles to see me. "Pssst..." I said it once more, waiting for the child to turn his head in my direction so that I could wave him toward me.

His bow tie hung crooked and his dirty blonde hair, which I'd gelled down only hours before, now stuck up in every direction, unruly curls descending over his face. He turned his head slowly, deep green eyes widening at the sight of me before the fading sun hit him square on the nose, spreading a soft light across the dash of freckles across his face. He squinted, trying to make me out properly. His little legs fidgeted as he restrained from stepping away from his assigned spot.

Cooper's mouth opened and then closed as I silently waved a finger in front of my lips, pleading with him to stay quiet. Turning the inside of my finger toward me, I extended it out so that I could gesture for him to join me.

It took only a brief moment before his feet found their freedom, and he ran toward me so quickly that I hardly had time to open my arms to him before he sailed into me. I smiled into his collar as he spoke.

"I thought maybe you were Dad!" he said in what I could only assume was his full-hearted effort at a whisper, although it truly ended up sounding more like a breathy squeal. "He bet me five dollars I couldn't stand still until the end of the ceremony, and I been just waitin' for him to try to make me lose."

"That does sound just like him, doesn't it? He's actually waiting for us in the car. How about the three of us get out of here?" I swung him onto my hip, not the least bit worried about smashing any of the lacy mess that covered me head to toe.

"What?" He made no effort to whisper this time.

I quickly took off in the direction of the car before we were noticed. It wouldn't do for anyone to see that the bride and groom, along with their son, were about to bail out of their own wedding. I wanted to be off of the estate property before word got out.

"Shh..." I said nothing else, moving toward our favorite spot by the water. Thankfully, it also happened to be far enough away from the wedding crowd that no one would hear or find us there.

"Are we going to the swing?" Cooper managed a real whisper this time, and the sweetness of it made me lean in to kiss him hard on his cheek. Still young enough not to have total disdain for his mother's affections, he smiled and laid his head against my shoulder.

"Yes, we are. I want to talk to you a minute. Just you and me, before we go join your dad. How'd you know I was taking you to the swing?"

"Don't you member that we always go there when we need *you and me* time at Grandfather's?"

"Of course, I remember. We've just really never discussed it, so I'm surprised you picked up on it."

"Yep. I did."

"I can see that. You're very smart for a four year old." And he was—exceedingly so. If it wasn't for Cooper's small size, most would guess him to be a good two years older.

"Yep, but I'm really four and seven months. That's almost five."

"My, and you're quite sure of yourself, too. That trait comes from your father."

"Yep."

By now, we'd reached what, in my opinion, was the most beautiful part of my parents' grand estate on Lake Placid. Nestled under a wide, broad-leafed tree that stood out among the many pine and spruce trees scattered throughout, hung a large white swing. It was built so that it hung perfectly from one of the tree's largest branches. Large cushions enveloped the floating chair. I collapsed into it, still holding Cooper as we fell back into the softness together.

I tugged playfully on one of his loose curls so that he'd look at me. "All right. Enough with the 'yeps.'" He giggled sheepishly at his orneriness. "I want to talk to you about something serious for a minute."

He scooted away from my arm so that he could regard me fully and, with all the determination he could muster, pulled the expression on his face into one of sheer seriousness. "I'm ready."

He regarded me sternly so I would get on with whatever it was I wished to discuss with him.

"Ok. What did you think about all of this today?"

His eyebrows scrunched together as if he were thinking very hard about how he should answer. I reached out to squeeze his hand, reassuring him that he could say whatever he wished. "I...I think it's weird."

"How do you mean, Coop? What was weird about it?"

"Well, I know that I'm only little, but I been thinkin' about this real hard."

I smiled, no doubt he had done just that. "I'm sure you have."

He glanced up at me beneath thick brown lashes, twirling his little fingers in nervous swirls before continuing. "And...I know Grandfather thinks moms and dads should be married, but I like things the way they are now. I heard something..."

He hesitated, gauging my reaction. He had a penchant for eavesdropping, and I could tell he worried I'd scold him for doing it again. "It's all right. What did you hear?'

"Last night, I heard Grams talking to Aunt Jane and Aunt Lily, and I didn't hear everything, but she said it was wrong of Grandfather to push you into this, Mom. That you and Dad liked each other too much to get married."

It sounded just like my mother. I only wished she'd said it to me and not my sisters. Perhaps I would've decided to call this thing off before the day of the actual wedding. "And what do you think about that?"

Cooper shrugged a little. "I think she's right, Mama. All Grams and Grandfather do is fight, and they're married. So do Aunt Lily and Uncle Jim. I don't want you and Pops to start fighting."

"Pops?" I laughed at the oddity of it. He'd never called Jeffrey 'Pops' once in his life.

"I heard Dad calling Bebop that and I liked it. Thought I would try it out."

"I see." I grinned, messing with his hair. "Well, I agree with you and so does 'Pops.' Your father and I can't get married. It wouldn't be fair of us to do that to this family. But that's why I wanted to talk to you; we *are* still a family. No matter whether me and your dad are married, the three of us are a family. Do you understand that?"

"Yes, Mom." He sighed, clearly believing that I had no reason to doubt his understanding. Honestly, I really didn't.

"And one more thing before we join your father. I don't want you to think that because you're little that I think less of what you think. If anything, I value what you think more than anyone else because you are little."

That...and I was slightly afraid he was already smarter than me. But I certainly wasn't going to say something like that to my son. I very much wanted him to think I was the smartest person on Earth for at least another decade.

"Ok, Mom. Can we go find Dad now?"

"Absolutely. Let's get out of here." Lifting Cooper out of the swing, I wrestled with the globs of white lace that gathered around me until I once again stood on two feet. Grabbing his hand, I peeked around the tree to make sure the coast was clear, and we took off, running toward the front of the house where his father waited with our escape vehicle.

"Are we going back to the City?" Cooper's words came out choppy, bouncing with every step of his short stride.

"For a minute we are, but I'll do even better. What's the one place you've always wanted to go?"

In that instant, his little feet stopped moving completely, and I nearly took a tumble with the jolt of the sudden stop.

"No! A plane? Oh Mama, am I *finally* gonna get to go on a plane?"

I laughed. He was four, nearly five truthfully, but still, how long could he really have been waiting? "Yes, you are. You're going to go on a job with me."

We neared the vehicle. Jeffrey must've seen us for he'd started the car and was awaiting our approach.

"Where are we goin'?"

"Scotland."

"Why?"

"I'll tell you in the car."

"*D*o you mind taking off your jacket so I can drape it over Coop?" I asked Jeffrey. "He's asleep. Can you hear him snoring?"

"Sweet sound, isn't it?" Jeffrey held his arm out to me so I would pull on his sleeve while he shrugged out of the tux jacket. Once free of it, I twisted so I could reach into the backseat and drape it over our sleeping son.

"He's the sweetest."

Once I faced the front of the car again, Jeffrey reached over to squeeze my shoulder. "We're getting close. Do you want to call the office to see if he's even there? It's pretty late."

I shook my head, confident that nothing much had changed in Mr. Perdie's routine since I took off work three days before for our wedding. "No, he'll be there. He works so much he wouldn't even come to the wedding, not that there was a wedding to come to, but you know what I mean."

"All right. Are you going to wear that?" He glanced at me, keeping one eye on the road.

"What are you saying? Do you think it's too much?" I laughed, but quickly silenced myself so I wouldn't wake Cooper. "Don't worry. He'll be the only one in the office at this hour, and he'll be so buried up to his elbows in work of some kind that I doubt he'll even take notice of the fact that I'm in a wedding gown. So yes, I am going to wear this. I need to talk to him before we do anything else to make sure it's all right that I start the job early."

For the first time since all of the wedding madness began a few days earlier, I thought about the new job. Mr. Perdie had come into my office literally an hour before I was due to take off for the next two weeks for my wedding. Apparently, an anonymous Scottish landowner had called Perdie, willing to donate a large sum of money to the magazine under the condition that we would do a lengthy piece on Scotland in an upcoming issue.

The call must have come as quite a shock to my boss. Not only did our readership seem to decline daily but, unbeknownst to the anonymous donor (or perhaps he knew quite well), our small travel magazine neared the brink of death. Only five more issues were guaranteed. The caller's donation would ensure that we could all keep our jobs for at least another five years.

Even more stunning, and the fact that had caused me to spill my sacred cup of coffee, was that the donor requested that *I* do the article. All of it. Writing. Photography. He specifically wanted me to author the piece.

I always worked hard, but being one of the newest photographers at the magazine, I'd never been given an assignment of significant value. I was usually allocated articles like *How To Pack Everything You Need For 10 Days In A Carry-On* and *Best Airport Restaurants*. As of yet, my only photography work had been photos of the inside of a suitcase and airport. Why the man would request that I do the article was beyond me.

After I'd overcome my initial shock, Perdie and I scheduled my trip for right after my honeymoon. But seeing as that would no longer happen, I saw no reason to wait another second. I imagined Mr. Perdie would feel the same, especially since receiving the donor's money was contingent upon my flight information being sent to him directly after its booking.

"Hey...where'd you go?" Jeffrey pulled into the parking garage below my office building and grasped my hand lightly to pull me from my reflective trance. "We're here."

"Sorry, I was just thinking about all of this. Crazy, isn't it?"

The corner of Jeffrey's brow pulled up quizzically, much like Cooper's had done earlier. They were so much alike in behavior and outward appearance that even I often had a hard time believing that they weren't actually biologically related.

"Which part, Grace? The 'you and me' bit, or this work stuff?"

I shrugged a bit, unbuckling and facing him as he slid into a parking spot and stopped the car. "All of it. Everything that seems to be going on." I reached out to grab both his hands. "I'm so sorry, Jeffrey. I can't express to you." I suddenly found myself quite choked up. "What it means...what it means that you've allowed me to pull you into all of this. And I don't just mean now. Always. Our whole lives it seems like I've been dragging you into one mess or another."

He frowned, pulling his hands free so he could cup both sides of my face. "You dragged me into nothing, Grace. Ever. Your father did when it came to law school and then joining his practice, but you never did. You're my best friend, and I consider you my closest family. There is nothing in this world I wouldn't do for you."

"Clearly." I smiled into his palms while thinking of the attire we were both wearing now. No matter how platonic our love for one another, he'd been willing to marry me at my father's request. "I love you, too. And gosh—Coop and I, we just couldn't do without you. Are you sure you're fine with me taking him along on the trip?"

Jeffrey released my face and glanced lovingly into the back seat of the car. "Absolutely. I'd come too, but I have one last case I have to finish before I rid myself of your father's firm. Coop will love every minute of it, and since we're going to delay his entry into kindergarten for a year, I have no problem with it."

"Good. Well, I guess I better go talk to my boss. Shouldn't take me long. Be back shortly."

It took me a good minute and a half to swing my feet out of the vehicle and gather the train and fabric that surrounded my legs and ankles. I moved rather self-consciously through the parking garage, although I went unseen. While I had no qualms about Mr. Perdie seeing me in my wedding regalia, I didn't really want anyone else wondering who the nut was roaming around in a gown.

I found my boss in his office, as expected. His glasses sat a bit crooked, and he had a mustard stain on his tie. Looking at him, I worried that he hadn't changed his clothes in the last three days. He was a kind enough man, but just glancing around his office caused a slight rise in my blood pressure. With organizational skills such as his, it was no wonder that the magazine struggled. I couldn't help wondering how many important things fell through the cracks in the black hole of Perdie's office.

"Mr. Perdie?"

He jerked up from his desk so quickly his chair flipped backward onto the floor. "Grace! What are you doing here? I mean, is everything all right? Of course, it mustn't be. You're still in your wedding dress."

He moved toward me quickly, and I instinctively reached out to grasp his hand in reassurance. "Yes, everything's fine. We just called it off, is all. Just drove in from—"

"What do you mean, everything's fine?" the small man asked shrilly, interrupting me. "Didn't you just say you called it off? That's rarely a good thing."

I was utterly shocked to see such concern from him, and it made me believe that perhaps I'd judged him wrongly for many years. "Yes, I promise. Everything is great. We just . . . we couldn't go through with it. Jeffrey and Cooper are waiting in the car, so it was really no tragedy or anything."

He patted my hand in a grandfatherly manner, although still a good many years off from being old enough to be anyone's grandfather. "That's good, Grace. Honestly, I've never really seen it between the two of you. It shocked me when you announced you were to be married."

I squeezed his hand in return, a sudden sensation of closeness growing between me and my quirky boss that I'd never felt before. "Well, Mr. Perdie, I must say I'm rather surprised by you. I never knew you to be so perceptive."

"Ms. Mitchell, perhaps it is you who lacks perception. I can assure you it's not a new quality I have developed. I know most of the time it appears that I can hardly keep my head screwed on, but I do notice almost everything."

I smiled and nodded before continuing on with the reason for my late night office visit. "I'd like to take on the Scotland job now and leave tomorrow, if that's all right. And..." I hesitated. It didn't truly matter whether or not he objected, but I still hoped he would have no problem with Cooper coming along for the trip. "Cooper is coming with me. I hope that won't be a problem."

"Of course you may start right away. As long as you complete the article and do a wonderful job of it, I have no problem with you bringing along your son. I believe we will have more than enough from our benefactor to pay for his flight, as well. I will book the flight for you both right away and will forward you the details when complete. Pack your bags, dear."

I nodded. "Thanks, Mr. Perdie."

As he turned toward his desk, I started to take my leave, but not before I heard his voice, laced with anxiety, follow me down the corridor. "And for the love of all things holy, Grace, do not screw this up. We'll be without our jobs by Christmas without this money."

CHAPTER 2

The Inn Near Conall Castle—Present Day

This time proved far easier than the last, but Eoghanan's scars still ached something dreadful. Each dab of the warm cloth that Morna pressed against the angry red line that now marked the entire length of his body caused him to grind his teeth to keep from screaming out.

"I'm sorry, lad, but I must first clean it before I place the salve upon it. Talk to me. It will help to distract ye from the pain a wee bit, though it must not be hurting ye as much as it did when ye first arrived here. Does it, Eoghanan?"

It took some effort to loosen his jaw enough to speak, but eventually he forced the words to come. "Nay, it doesna hurt as much as then, but if I were standing, it would do a fair job of bringing me to my knees all the same." The old witch was right, releasing the tight clench of his jaw did seem to ease the pain a little, or at least it helped him to notice it less. He thought it best

11

to keep talking. "I saw her again. The same lass as the last time. Her and the wee lad both."

"Ah, and what lass is this?"

Morna's voice gave nothing away, but her hand momentarily stilled along the side of his neck, all but confirming what he suspected. She already knew the woman of whom he spoke.

He cocked a brow and looked her square in the eye. "Ye know the lass far better than I, doona ye? I've only watched her, but ye have sent me to her twice."

This time the old woman remained entirely unbothered, continuing her slow and steady cleansing of his injured side. "I doona wish to disappoint ye, but I am not familiar with the lass, and I have sent ye nowhere, lad. 'Tis not the way this magic works."

Eoghanan struggled to sit up, but was restrained by Morna's hand moving to press his shoulder back down onto the bed, causing his frustration to rise even further. "I doona believe ye. Is it not yer magic that not only brought me here but sends me back now? What I canna figure out is the purpose behind it. Why not send me back to a time earlier, but still in this verra spot, if I canna yet go home? I doona know where I have been the last two times, but it wasna Scotland. I'd bet my verra life on that fact."

Eoghanan watched as resignation washed over his bed nurse. The lines of her face softened slightly. He hoped answers might finally be given to him.

"Ach, ye are a stubborn lad, are ye not? But still...I suppose ye deserve an explanation." She pulled the cloth away from the top of Eoghanan's shoulder, dipping it into the water then reaching over the basin beside her to ring it out before draping it over the side of the bowl. Hands free, she leaned back in her seat, crossing her arms. "I'll not lay blame on myself for not providing ye one earlier, though. Ye were in such a rush to travel back to yer home that ye wouldna have listened to anything that I said. Ye dinna even allow me the chance to tell ye that yer first travel wouldna be to the time ye wished it."

Eoghanan succeeded in sitting up this time, determined to look at Morna straight on as she spoke to him. His red hair hung in his face, covering his green eyes and frustrating him. He blew the strands upward to clear his vision. "Aye, I am in a hurry to return home. My brother's wife is with child, and I doona wish to miss the bairn's arrival. I have stayed too long here."

Morna's head shook forcefully in denial of what he'd said. "No. Ye havena stayed nearly long enough. Do ye not remember what happened to ye the first time I sent ye back? Why, yer wound split partially open, and ye nearly died...again! If I were ye, I wouldna wish to go knocking on death's door another time. Ye probably havena heard it, but there's something people say in this time—third time's a charm. Ye go visiting death again, and he might just decide to answer the door." She paused momentarily, lowering her voice which had grown rather excited. "That being said, I will do all I can to make sure ye will be strong enough to return home before the child's arrival. But in order for ye to be so, we must keep working to send ye back, but not so far so quickly."

A fortnight earlier, after spending months nearly entirely bedridden, Morna's announcement that she was ready to use her magic on him had indeed excited him so much that he'd not allowed any further instruction or explanation. He demanded that she use it on him at once.

The result was an experience so shocking and strange that Eoghanan still could not fully process all that he'd seen, only holding on to the one piece of serenity he'd found in the chaotic world he'd been sent to—the beautiful lass and the young boy by her side.

For as the spell had begun, Eoghanan expected to arrive back on the shore of McMillan Castle's lake in precisely the same year he'd left—1647. Instead he'd landed in a frightening and very noisy jungle filled with tall structures and foul smells. Thankfully, he awoke in the shadows and went unnoticed, free to observe the oddities so foreign from all he'd ever known.

Pushing thoughts of the experience aside for a moment, he returned to the conversation at hand. "Aye, I doona wish to meet death any time soon. I do wish, however, that ye'd silenced me long enough to warn me of what I would see. I'd like to think that I am not a man easily frightened, but arriving in a place so different from what I expected was--" His lack of comprehension stopped him. "It was verra unsettling. But never mind. Tell me about the magic, for if ye doona keep sending me to the same lass, why is it that I end up in her presence each time?"

Morna sat quietly for a moment. Eoghanan assumed she wondered how best to try to explain it to him. Eventually, she asked, "Do ye remember the stone that brought ye here?"

He nodded, though the memory was a vague one. There'd not been much life in him when he traveled forward. "Aye, I do. What of it?"

"That stone is verra much my own magic—created by me for the use of yer sister-in-law, Mitsy, and now for yerself. But the stone is tied directly to one location and time—yer own. I know enough of how the time travel works and what it does to one's body, essentially ripping ye fair apart before placing ye back together again, to know that yer wounds were not healed enough to take ye all the way back that many centuries. I thought it best to use spells already in place for many years, created by others with magic, to allow ye to build up yer strength before such a long trip. They allow me to decide just how far back I wish ye to go, but there are powers greater than my own that choose just exactly where ye end up."

Eoghanan's brows pulled in, displaying his doubt before he had a chance to mask it. "And just what powers are these?"

"I suppose everyone thinks of such a power differently. Ye could call it fate, I suppose. Perhaps, ye are meant to know the lass?"

"No, though she is a lovely sight to be sure, I willna be here long enough to know anyone, save ye and yer husband, Jerry."

Morna said nothing, merely reaching back to grab the cloth, rinsing it once more before gesturing to him to lay back again. "Let me tell ye now how I plan to build up yer strength so there will be no more questions about me being truthful with ye. The first time, ye were only sent back three months in time, and it was too far. This last time was doable, only a week back, but as it still caused ye some pain, I think it best if today's journey only takes ye back a few hours—a day at the most. Tomorrow we shall go a bit farther, a week and a half, I reckon, and then the next day a bit shorter, and so on and so on. One day far, one day close, until we build up yer strength. Is this acceptable to ye?"

Eoghanan winced as the cloth touched his tender skin once more, his voice slightly unsteady as he answered, "Aye, 'tis fine."

Morna smiled at him, squeezing his hand in sympathy before pressing the rag against him once more. "I'm only just to yer shoulder. After I've cleansed ye, I still have to apply the salve. Best ye tell me about this lass ye have seen. Ye havena spoken of her until today."

"Verra well." He'd thought of nothing else for days, so despite Morna's request, it seemed the only natural thing of which to speak. Besides, he'd not yet been given the opportunity to write about her and all he'd seen, a practice he'd kept religiously since childhood. He didn't want to forget her. Perhaps speaking of the lass would keep her fresh in his memory so he would have the words ready when it came time to write. "I doona know her name. The wee boy, her son I suppose, calls her 'Mom.' The lad is called Cooper. An odd name to be sure, but it seems to fit him just fine."

Once he started, the words left him freely, and Eoghanan took his time describing every instant, recalling every word he'd heard between the woman and the boy. He no longer spoke directly to Morna, but more to himself. It stirred something inside him to speak of the lass and her son, something that made him feel alive and whole rather than the weak, wounded man he'd been for the past many moons.

The memories of his beloved strangers took him away. He no longer felt the witch's work, and didn't notice that she'd finished tending to his wounds until he heard Jerry's voice in the doorway.

"Morna dear, when ye are finished with him, will ye join me? I need some help in the garden if ye doona mind. There's a wee beasty weed that is near strangling the life out of one of my plants. I'd like ye to use a bit of magic and kill the devil."

Patting Eoghanan's hand in a motherly fashion, Morna stood from her place beside him, glancing over her shoulder to answer her husband. "I'm finished here. I'll leave the lad to rest a while and we will try out another travel this afternoon." She returned her attention to Eoghanan. "Are ye comfortable? Will ye be okay for a few hours?"

Eoghanan nodded confidently. "Aye, but I'd like to write in my book. Could ye hand it to me?"

Morna started in the direction of his journal but stopped midway, turning a mischievous smile at him. "No, I doona think so. Ye need to start building yer strength. Walking across the room willna rip ye open from temple to toe. I'll leave ye to get it for yerself."

* * *

*J*erry grasped at Morna's arm as soon as she closed the bedroom door behind her. "Ye are much too good at making up lies, love. It unsettles me a bit."

Morna looked at him incredulously. "I doona know what ye mean by that."

He stopped and faced her, blocking her path down the hallway, staring at her with one wiry eyebrow raised. When she smiled guiltily, he said, "Ach, look there. See, ye do know perfectly what I mean. Ye told that lad that ye doona choose where he ends up. If that were true, I wouldna have had to speak to a Mr. Perdie in America about the money that we will give him to get the lass here, would I?"

"Have ye taken to spying on me, Jerry?"

"I've always spied on ye. Ye get yerself in far too much trouble without my supervision. But I doona believe I knew until today just how well ye could lie."

His wife leaned in to kiss him reassuringly on the cheek. "Life isna worth it without some trouble now and then, but ye shouldna be surprised that I am a good liar. 'Tis a trait of women and the fault of men that we must be so. Yer folly has required it of us. I dare ye to find one woman that isna capable of it."

Giving his cheek a quick pat, Morna pushed past him and made her way down the hall, leaving Jerry stunned and open-mouthed.

CHAPTER 3

LaGuardia Airport, New York City—Present Day

An hour spent in line at airport security, mixed with the general hectic chaos of the airport, was enough to put a damper on the anticipation of even the most enthusiastic traveler. For all his excitement, by the time we finally sat down at our gate to await boarding, Cooper had mellowed dramatically from the bouncy, ecstatic boy he'd been earlier in the morning.

"Are you nervous?" I nudged him lightly with my elbow, eliciting a trademark lift of an eyebrow as he squirmed in his seat to face me.

"Nah. Why would I be nervous? I've always wanted to fly. I was born to fly, Mama."

I chuckled, glancing down at my watch to check the time. "Oh, you were, huh? Well, you'll get to shortly. Only an hour until takeoff now. I bet we start boarding within the next fifteen minutes or so."

"Fifteen?" For a brief second his voice held a slight whine, but he checked it quickly, knowing it wouldn't be tolerated. "I don't think I can wait for even five." He held up four fingers, but silently counted as he looked over his hand and quickly extended his thumb so it displayed the correct number.

"Oh, I bet you can. Let's do something to pass the time. Want to work on your reading?" He loved for me to read to him. It was no surprise he was catching on quickly.

Enthused, he immediately reached to the floor to grab his backpack so he could make a reading choice.

"Can we read the book Dad gave me last night?"

"Sure." I responded reflexively, but I watched him rummage through his bag apprehensively. Jeffrey was in no way much of a reader. I couldn't, for the life of me, imagine Jeffrey going to a bookstore to find a book for Cooper. I anticipated him pulling a comic out of his backpack. That was fine. It just wouldn't be the reading material I knew Cooper would want. He didn't enjoy pop-up and sticker books; he wanted more words than pictures. Just another trait that made him anything but the typical child.

"This one."

Surprising me, he extended *The Little Prince* by Antoine de Saint-Exupéry. So much more than a simplistic children's story, this tale had just the sort of depth that Cooper would enjoy. Although I would have to explain some of the meaning to him, he wouldn't mind. He loved to learn.

"Dad gave this to you?" I couldn't mask the doubt in my voice.

"Yeah, but Bebop helped. Dad said that since the two of you were getting so many gifts for the wedding, I needed something, too. He said he didn't know what to get me, but then Bebop helped."

That made much more sense. It was Cooper's Bebop, Jeffrey's dad, who'd introduced me to the story when I was a little girl. A warm, funny, and caring man so different from my own father, I'd spent most of my childhood wishing I'd been born to him instead.

"Ah, well, this is a very special gift, ya know? It's one of my favorites."

"Really?" I'd drawn him in now. Knowing that I loved the book, he'd sit contently and listen to me read it even if he didn't care for it, although I knew he would.

"Yes, really. Scoot in closer and I'll start. I don't think this is the best book for us to practice your own reading with though. It's a bit long."

He pulled his feet up into the seat and slid in tight, leaning toward me. "That's fine. I'll just listen."

He smiled, leaning his head against my shoulder as my heart squeezed happily. I'd just opened the cover when we were interrupted by an attendant alerting all those at our gate that boarding would begin promptly.

"Ope!" I made the excited noise as I closed the spine and slid the book back into his backpack. "This is it, Coop. We'll read it on the plane, okay?"

"Okay."

His legs flew off the seat so fast he just about fell down. Catching himself, he threw his backpack on and smiled ecstatically, as happy as I'd ever seen him.

Thrilled as he was, he flatly refused to board with the group "travelers with small children." While I would've enjoyed the benefit of getting on the plane first, I didn't push the issue. I wouldn't deny him anything that brought him this much joy.

Once all the pre-boarders left the gate area, we lined up with the rest, squished firmly somewhere in between groups B and C. Cooper held my hand tightly, leaning out past the line so he could see something besides the backsides of those in front of us.

I watched him smiling, when suddenly he jerked away from me, spinning to face something catty-corner from the line where he waved a little shyly. Startled, I crouched down next to him, placing my hand on his shoulder so I could steady myself while I looked in the same direction. I could see no one—no one that either of us knew, at least.

"What are you waving at?" I lightly squeezed his shoulder to pull his attention away from who or what had captured his focus.

"Over there." He pointed to the side of an escalator where a shadow spread deep over the tile around it. "Do you remember the man I told you about at the park? With the scars? He's here again."

Grateful that I'd steadied myself with his shoulder, I spun him toward me, doing my best to keep my voice calm despite the shiver that shook me all over. "I remember you mentioning the man, but I never saw him. Are you sure he's here now?"

I released my grip so he could turn and look again, and I tried to do the same. Again, I saw no one. Cooper met my gaze, clearly frustrated. "He's not there anymore, but he was. I know it."

He never lied. Even when he tried to, he could only last a few seconds before his face would give way with guilt and he would fess up. If he believed he saw someone, he meant it, but why had I not noticed the man, as well?

Sure, I had a lot on my mind lately—my almost-wedding and new job—not to mention that, like every mother, half of my mind always rested on Cooper. Still, it seemed that every time I attempted to look at the man Cooper mentioned, the stranger vanished into thin air. I couldn't help but wonder if Cooper saw someone who wasn't really there. An imaginary friend, perhaps? As the line started to move, I decided to direct my questioning to that effect.

"So, what's your new friend's name?"

He looked up at me with a face that plainly relayed that he thought I'd lost my mind. "I don't know him, Mom. I don't know his name."

He shook his head at me, apparently astonished at my stupidity.

"Well, then why did you wave at him?"

He shrugged, lifting my hand a little. "He looked sad, and he looked right at me, just like at the park."

The thought made me uneasy. "You said he has bad scars? Does he scare you?"

"No." He seemed surprised by my suggestion. "He's not a bad guy just because he has scars, Mom."

"Of course not," I muttered quickly, instantly regretting the implication of my question. "I just meant—" *What did I mean?* "He's a stranger. How do you know he's not scary?"

He shrugged his little shoulders and we moved forward a step in the line. "Bebop says even if somebody is smiling, you can see meanness in their eyes." He paused a moment and I said nothing, knowing by his held breath that he wasn't finished speaking. "And I think he's right. Just look at Grandfather. He smiles at people all the time, but he's not very nice."

I looked down at him, unsure of what to say. It seemed wrong to let him speak poorly of my father, but I could hardly disagree with him. Instead, I chose to direct the conversation back to the stranger. "So this man's eyes weren't mean, huh?"

"Nope. I think he likes us, Mom."

We neared the gate, and I extended Cooper's boarding pass toward him so he could hand it to the attendant to scan. "Well, why wouldn't he like us? Here—do you want to hand it to her?"

"Yes!" He snatched the pass from me and leaned to the side to see how close we were to the front of the line. "We're almost there, we're almost there. You can let go of my hand now if you want, Mom."

I released his hand, stepping behind him so he could have his ticket checked first. After both our tickets were scanned, I stayed a half-step behind him, allowing him to lead us into the makeshift hallway leading toward the plane. He all but bounced up and down with the excitement radiating off him.

His happiness did me good and, for a moment, I forgot all about Cooper's mysterious stranger until a quick glance down at my bag made me realize I'd left my jacket draped over the chair where Cooper and I had been sitting.

Calling to him to stop, I waved him toward me. "Hey, I want you to wait right here. I left my coat. I'm just going to go ask the attendant if she'll grab it for me."

He nodded, trying to hide his disappointment that we would move back a few places in the line to get on the plane.

Squeezing his hand, I stepped away and hurried back up the ramp, pushing my way against the flow of people until I stood next to the gate entry, making sure not to step back outside of it. "Miss..." I reached out to tap the girl on the shoulder. "I'm so sorry, I believe I left my jacket on that chair over there." I pointed in the direction of the chair, but couldn't see it due to the line. "Would you mind grabbing it for me?"

To my surprise, she extended the light cotton jacket in my direction. "Is it this one?"

"Why, yes." I reached out for it, surprised it had been noticed amongst the crowd of people. "Did a passenger pick it up?"

She shook her head and jerked it to the side. "Not a passenger on this plane. He must have been waiting at another gate. He just laid it over the counter here and turned to walk away before I could speak to him."

"Which way did he go?" I looked around the mass of people, trying to find the man.

"I don't know. I'm a bit busy, as you can see." The woman smiled, but clearly she wished for me to leave now. Although there was no way for me to know for sure that Cooper's stranger was the man who'd retrieved my jacket, he was very much on my mind.

CHAPTER 4

The Inn Near Conall Castle—Present Day

Overnight flights are meant to be slept on, but try as I might to explain this concept to Cooper, he had none of it. While he still operated with the same inexhaustible amount of energy he had maintained aboard the flight, the full effects of jet lag crashed down on me hard, making me ill-tempered.

"Mr. Perdie, there's no way this is where I'm supposed to stay. I know you said it was an inn, but there's no sign or anything. It's in the middle of nowhere. Why on earth would an inn set up here?"

I fumbled with the GPS system with one hand, holding my phone to my ear with the other. While Perdie read aloud the coordinates, I frowned down at the navigation screen in frustration. "Yes, that's exactly where I am, but this...this just can't be it."

"Mom, look!" Cooper's voice, loud, high, and demanding sounded as pleasing to my tired ears as an out of tune oboe.

"Coop," I snapped a little too harshly. "What have I told you about interrupting when I'm on the phone? You have to wait until I'm finished."

"But..." his voice quivered. "There's a man at the door. He's wav...waving." His voice broke completely as he finished explaining, and my heart broke with it.

I hurried off the phone with Mr. Perdie, mumbling something along the lines of, "Nevermind, I'll call you later," before hurrying to apologize to my son. "I'm sorry. I shouldn't have yelled at you. I'm just exhausted. No sleep turns me into a scary troll."

"A very scary troll," he said.

Although he wasn't ready to smile at me, I knew I'd been forgiven. "Now, what's this about a man? I don't see anybody." *Again,* I thought to myself. It worried me that twice in the course of twenty-four hours Cooper had seen someone I hadn't. Although I wasn't sure which one of us I should be worried for— him for his overactive imagination, or myself for my horrifying lack of observational skills. I guessed we would find out soon enough.

Cooper threw his hands up in exasperation. "Well, that's because he went back inside. He waved real big and then," he pulled his hand toward his chest, demonstrating the man's hand motion, "he wants us to come inside, too."

I put the car in drive and turned off the main road. Parking in front of the inn, I turned off the engine. "All right. I'll take your word for it. Let's leave our bags here, just in case, okay?"

Unbuckling his seatbelt, Cooper nodded before reaching to open the car door, popping the handle with his fingers and then kicking it open the rest of the way with his feet. Once outside, he slammed the door as hard as he could, which was just hard enough to close the door properly.

Anxious to greet the man who'd waved to him, Cooper knocked on the front door before I reached his side. As I neared him, the door swung open, revealing an ancient-looking man who looked so grumpy I could scarcely imagine that this was the man Cooper thought had waved us inside.

Much to my astonishment, the stranger's face altered completely in the next second. His large, warm smile contrasted vastly with his scowl of only moments before. That might've unsettled me normally, but the old man now appeared so welcoming that both Cooper and I couldn't help but smile in return.

He extended a large, bony hand and Cooper reached out with confidence to grasp it firmly—perhaps the one good thing my father had taught him.

"Why, good morning, lad. We've been expecting ye. I am Jerry. I believe my wife has prepared some brunch for ye both. Why doona ye come in?" The man looked up at me and smiled before returning his attention to Cooper. "And who might this lovely lass standing behind ye be?"

Cooper reached his left hand behind him, extending it in my direction so I would take it, effectively presenting me to the man. When he wished to be, Coop had it in him to be quite the little gentleman.

"This is my mom."

The man, Jerry, stepped forward. I moved to extend my own hand, but instead he clasped me on the shoulder, ushering us inside. "Aye, I reckoned she was, though she looks young enough to be yer sister. What is yer name, laddie, and how old are ye?"

Continuing to move down the hall in the direction Jerry indicated, Cooper occasionally glanced behind him so he could look at Jerry as he spoke. "I'm Cooper. I'm four years old, but not really four because I'll be five very soon."

"Ach, I'd have guessed ye a fair deal older than that, laddie."

Cooper nodded, clearly expecting this response. "Yeah, everybody says that."

"And ye..." Jerry lowered his voice so that I knew he now spoke to me and not Cooper, "must be Grace, aye?"

I nodded, battling a brief moment of confusion. The reservation must have required something more than the name of the magazine for him to know my first name. I knew for certain I hadn't been given the chance to introduce myself yet.

We stepped into the kitchen, and while the smell was enough to alert us that someone had been busy cooking, the room was empty. Still, Jerry ushered us inside.

"Go on and have a seat, the both of ye. I believe my wife has gone upstairs to invite our other guest down for a meal. Though he usually dines in his room, I expect he'd like to meet the two of ye."

"Why?" I asked the question before I had a chance to check it, but I didn't understand his conclusion. If I were staying at an inn, I certainly wouldn't feel the need to meet and greet every new guest that checked in.

"Ach, well," the old man seemed slightly rattled by my question, or perhaps the bluntness of it. "He's been here several months now, and the two of ye are the first guests we've had since he arrived. I expect my wife thinks 'twould do him good to see some other people."

"Don't you think a grown man can decide for himself what would do him good? Why has he been here so long? It certainly doesn't look like there would be much to do around here." I surprised myself once again with my frankness. Usually, I wasn't so blunt, but something about the situation and the conversation felt very odd to me, and I couldn't help but continue my inquiry.

"Why, lass, I just offered ye food. Why ye feel the need to berate me so, I doona know. Both of yer questions ye can ask the lad yerself when he gets down here. Now, sit." He pointed at a chair to his left.

I did as he bid, ashamed at my lack of manners. "I'm sorry. I'm afraid jet lag is hitting me rather hard. I appreciate the food. We both do."

Jerry patted and squeezed my shoulder once again. "Doona

worry about it, lass. Travel is a tough business. Ye two help yerself to the food. I'll go see if my wife needs some help." He slipped quickly away.

Before I could gather the energy to stand, I glanced over to see Cooper on his tiptoes, trying to reach the eggs on the stove, about to dump them onto the floor.

Leaping from my seat, I used the last of my energy reserves to reach for the tilting plate.

"How do ye feel, lad?"

Morna's voice next to his bedside worried Eoghanan. Perhaps the travel had injured him, though as he lay with his eyes closed, he felt no more pain than usual. Each time, the journey made his head ache and his wounds burn. But all in all, he sensed less pain than the previous times.

He jerked his eyes open, adjusting to the bright light above him, working to collect himself from the slight confusion that followed each journey before finally looking in Morna's direction.

"I feel better than before, though my head aches as it always does."

"Aye, I'm afraid there's no way around that bit of it. Do ye feel like rising from yer bed for a while? We have new visitors who will be staying with us. I think it polite if ye come and meet them. Ye are bound to bump into one another over the next few weeks."

Her words surprised him. Not a soul had happened across his host's home since his arrival. So many days spent in near solitude made him doubt his ability to communicate suitably, especially if the visitors were from the time he found himself in now. "No, thank ye, Morna. I think it best that I rest a while more."

The look on Morna's face confirmed his fears. She'd not meant it as a real question. Throwing a bundle of strange clothes toward him, she said, "I dinna ask ye for ye to say no. Now, ye can either get up, or I shall drag ye up, but downstairs to the kitchen ye shall go, one way or the other."

Resigned, Eoghanan slowly swung his legs over the side of the bed and sat up. He was thankful that the task of moving about normally became easier with each passing day. "Fine. I dinna think ye would let me stay here, but I thought it worth a try."

"Ye knew it fruitless to try before ye uttered the words. Now put these on. Ye canna wear the loose linen ye have on now, for no man would wear it in this time. I have tried to find ye the lightest modern material I could, so it willna press too much against yer side, but no doubt ye will feel it against the scar."

Eoghanan held up both garments. The first, while about the length of a kilt, was made of a fabric he'd never seen before and had two holes, one for each of his legs, he assumed. The top scrunched together and, as he pulled on the sides, he watched in fascination as the bottoms grew and shrunk with his efforts. "And what are these, Morna?"

"I believe that American men wear them while they play sports. Jerry said he's seen basketball players don them. I thought that since the waistband is moveable, it would hurt less than placing ye in a pair of fitted pants."

Eoghanan frowned down at the garments. "Men must take no pride in how they look to wear such ridiculous clothing. Can I not just wear my kilt?"

"It's too heavy just yet. It would rub against yer scars. Just strip yer clothes, and I'll help ye. Doona be shy about it, either. All these months of healing ye, I've seen every blessed inch of ye, and ye know it well."

Not a skilled talker on his best day, Eoghanan knew the witch would win every war of words with him. He stood to step out of the thin linen pants, deciding not to argue the point further. His mind took him, instead, back to where he'd been only moments before. "The lad saw me this time. I know he did. I suspected he did the first time, but I couldna be sure. This time, he waved at me."

He thought back on the boy, smiling and waving at him as if he'd known him all his young life.

"Oh?" Morna lifted his foot to slide it into a solid white covering she called a 'tennis-shoe.' "I'll not say that it surprises me that a child was the one to see ye. They are much more perceptive than adults."

"Aye, I believe the boy to be verra wise for his small age. He dinna seem to be afraid of the way I look." Eoghanan tried to wiggle his toes, grimacing at the monstrosity being strapped to his foot.

"Why would he be? Ye look mighty fine in my eyes, and I'd be hard pressed to find any lass that dinna think ye so."

He pulled up one corner of his mouth in disagreement. "Mayhap once, but not so much anymore. I doona mind it, but 'tis true well enough."

"Hogwash." Morna swatted his covered foot dismissively. "Yer scars may look a bit painful now, but as they fade, they will only draw lassies to ye, wait and see. Makes ye look a wee bit dangerous, and I doona know any lass that doesna like a bit of danger in a man, whether she is willing to admit it or not. No matter that ye are about as dangerous as a wee kitten, ye willna look that way, and that's what matters."

"If ye say so. Are ye done with me? I feel rather foolish."

In answer to his question, Morna stood from her crouching place at his feet. "Aye. Ye know ye seemed surprised that the child wasna scared of the way ye looked. Children are only afraid of what they're taught to be afraid of." She paused and opened the bedroom door, motioning toward him to follow her into the hallway. "'Tis a credit to the boy's mother that he wasna bothered by ye. It means she's taught him to look at more than a person's appearance."

Eoghanan followed Morna down the stairs and into the

hallway. Mention of the lad's mother made him think back to the way her garment had felt in his hands and the risk he'd taken by going after it once she'd left it. It smelled lovely, and he could imagine holding her in his arms. He had almost wished to keep the garment for himself but instead had left it for her, quickly rushing back to his place in the shadows. He could almost smell it now, the same scent he'd noticed on the covering. The fragrance was so lifelike in his memory, he found himself bewildered by it. How could he smell something so strongly when it wasn't there?

He stepped into the kitchen to greet the inn's new guests and went still. The scent that he thought only lingered in his memory now clung to the very woman he had been thinking about. She stood before him. Both she and the young lad.

CHAPTER 5

"Hey, I know you. Did you get on the same plane as us?" Cooper blurted.

I'd just set him down at the kitchen table with a plate full of eggs and some sort of weird sausage I had no intention of eating when his exclamation caused me to glance up. Jerry's wife stood in the doorway alongside the inn's other resident.

At the sight of the man, I understood Cooper's words immediately, and the room suddenly seemed to grow quite small. I reached behind to steady myself but found that I groped at nothing but air.

Jerry's hand found mine as he stepped to my side. "Are ye all right, lass?"

I nodded as he led me to a chair next to Cooper.

"She's just a bit tired is all," Jerry said, speaking on my behalf. "Verra long trip from America. I think some sleep would do her good."

"Well, she canna sleep yet," said Jerry's wife. "Her inner clock will be totally awry if she goes to sleep now. She must at least make it through the day before resting." The woman stepped

33

toward me in greeting, placing her hand on my shoulder, much as Jerry had done. "I'm Morna. I'll get ye some coffee."

I said nothing to her as I continued to stare at the man who remained in the doorway. Scars or not, this couldn't be the person Cooper believed he saw. The attendant had said the man wasn't on our flight. Even if he had been, how could he have beaten us here? We'd been shuttled straight from the airport to the car rental, and had driven from there to here immediately. Besides, Jerry had said this man had been a guest at the inn for months.

Allowing myself to rationalize the man's presence and Cooper's reaction to him as a simple case of mistaken identity, I allowed myself to look him over without such a sense of overwhelming alarm. Much like the stranger Cooper had described, I found nothing about this man's appearance frightening, although intimidating was another matter entirely.

Despite his ridiculous outfit of stark white tennis shoes, socks that went halfway up his calves, black athletic shorts, and a simple white undershirt, he exuded such confident masculinity it made something within my veins hum to life with an awareness of him. He filled the width of the doorway with his wide shoulders and was tall enough to have to crouch in order to pass underneath it. I imagined he stood at least six feet five, and despite being quite lean in stature, I guessed him to weigh a good two hundred and sixty pounds—all muscle.

His eyes were shockingly green, highlighted by specks of gold that seemed to reflect light in a way that made his eyes stand out amongst the mass of red hair that reached his shoulders. His state of dress made little sense to me; there was such a raw masculinity to him, a note of pride and refinement to the way he carried himself. I couldn't imagine him willingly wearing such an odd, laid-back outfit on a day-to-day basis.

Only when I tore my gaze away from his eyes and focused on the scar that ran from the top of his temple on his right side, all the way down to the top of his sock, did I understand the garb.

He didn't bear the scars of an old wound, but a new one. They were still fresh—pink and angry in their appearance, still soft and, I supposed, very much still sore.

Cooper's voice startled me, and I glanced down at the plate Morna placed in front of me with embarrassment. I'd unapologetically been staring the man down, most likely the last thing he needed after whatever horrible thing had happened to him to cause such a wound.

"Hey, mister, didn't you hear what I said? Did you come here on the same plane? What's your name?"

I glanced up from my plate with reddened cheeks and watched closely the man's reaction to my son. He, too, seemed to have to pull himself away from something. Only then did I realize that he'd been studying me just as closely as I had him.

He coughed into a clenched fist, seemingly to find his voice, and took a step into the kitchen, pulling himself up to his full height for the first time. Looking at Cooper, he shook his head and smiled. "No, I dinna. My name is Eoghanan. What shall I call ye, lad?"

Cooper beamed at the oddity of the man's name. Pushing himself away from the table, he stood and approached Eoghanan, who towered over him.

"Yo-yu-what? My name is Cooper."

He stuck his hand out toward the man who took it gladly, allowing Cooper to shake it far longer than was customary. At least the man seemed to have patience when it came to children. That said something about his character.

The man announced his name again, only a little more slowly, making it sound even more unusual. Cooper couldn't refrain from giggling.

"I've never heard a name like that before. Yo-yun...yo-yun..." Cooper fumbled with the strange syllables before finally throwing his hands up in exasperation. "I give up. How about I just call you E-o? Would that be okay?"

E-o, as my son renamed him, let loose a smile so bright that it seemed to ease some of the tension in the room. His deep laughter made everyone smile in curious wonderment at what he found so funny.

Cooper seemed especially intent on finding out. "What's so funny? I just gave you a nickname, is all. Lots of people have those. Mine is Coop. Mama calls me that a lot. You can call me that if you want to, too. That, or just Cooper, I don't mind either one."

Now free from my son's handshake, Eoghanan moved across the room to fill his own plate, speaking with his back toward us as he did so. "'Tis only that yer 'nickname,' as ye called it, made me think of someone verra dear. She, too, has trouble with my name and decided on the same name as ye have, lad. And, aye, ye may call me E-o for I know she wouldna mind sharing it with ye."

With his plate full, he joined us at the table, sitting next to Morna and across from Cooper and me, with Jerry rounding out the table by sitting at its head. The table was smaller than what one would find at the average restaurant. As a result, the five of us found ourselves sitting in very close proximity. No matter that most of us were strangers to one another, I found it impossible to behave as such due to the familiar way in which we sat, and I unthinkingly blurted out the first thing that came to mind.

"The woman who called you by the same name—was she a girlfriend? Or an ex-wife, perhaps?" The questions slipped out, and I groaned internally. It was absolutely none of my business. Apparently, lack of sleep had the remarkable ability to loosen my tongue. It no longer seemed safe for me to be in the presence of those I might insult, so I decided it was time that Cooper and I leave to explore the area for the rest of the day—just as soon as we finished our meal.

With an even deeper blush than before, I raised my eyes to see a look of amusement on the man's face.

"I doona believe that I know yer name, lass."

"I...I'm sorry. It's . . . I'm Grace." I set down my fork and held out a hand in between stuttered words. He took my fingertips into his hand, kissing my knuckles before pulling away and directing his attention back to his food.

"'Tis a pleasure to meet ye, Grace. Aye, the lass is the bonniest of girlfriends. Can one have an ex-wife as ye said? I doona know, but she is not my wife. She is my brother's."

"Ah." The noise made little sense, but neither did his explanation. Either he didn't understand what a girlfriend was, or he'd just gleefully confessed to dating his sister-in-law. And, to my knowledge, there were few places left in the world that didn't allow some sort of spousal separation. Perhaps it was his way of making some sort of joke I didn't get. I very much hoped he wasn't a comedian.

Not wishing to delve further into that can of worms, I finished my food as quickly as possible and waited patiently for Cooper to do the same. Once he'd clearly had his fill, I stood, scooping up both our plates so that I could rinse them, only stopping at Morna's insistence.

"If ye know what's best for ye, lass, ye will leave those dishes be right this instant. No guest of mine will ever clean a dish if I have anything to say about it. Why doona ye go with Jerry, and he'll help ye carry yer bags to yer room and allow ye some time to settle in?"

Obeying, I left the dishes inside the sink, turning so I could properly address her. "Thank you, but I think we'll wait to get our bags if that's all right. I'd like to go ahead and scope out the lay of the land and decide just what I want to work on photographing tomorrow."

Morna stood as Cooper hopped down from his seat to make his way over to me. "Aye, o'course. The two of ye are free to do as ye wish."

"Okay, great. We will be back sometime this afternoon. Thank you for the food. It was delicious." I reached to rub my fingers through Cooper's hair as he approached me. "Wasn't it, Coop? You ready?"

"Yep, but can I ask E-o something first?"

A scary question coming from someone as inquisitive as Cooper, but I didn't imagine there was much chance of him asking something as intrusive as I had. "I don't mind, but it's up to him whether or not he answers your question."

Eoghanan smiled. "Ask whatever ye wish, lad. I'll answer ye."

"If you didn't come here on the plane with us, did you fly in on a spaceship? 'Cause I know you're the same man I saw at the playground and at the airport." Astonishingly, he didn't smile or laugh as he asked. He meant it as an entirely serious question.

"What? Cooper, why would you ask him that?" I answered in Eoghanan's place, wishing to spare him the oncoming conversation.

"Maybe he's like the little prince in the book, Mom. He flies around to different places like the little prince did to different planets."

"Oh, I see." Realization dawned on me as I remembered our flight time story. At least Cooper was making text-to-world connections, regardless of how far-fetched they might be. "Coop, you know that was just a story, right?"

He twisted, crossing his arms as he looked up at me, disappointed. "Man, Mom. I guess that means you're a real grown-up. Only a grown-up would say it was just a story. Don't you remember the problem with grown-ups from the book? Kids see things more clearly."

This would require a longer conversation than I was willing to have in front of our captive audience. "Often times they do, Coop, but I don't think your new friend is the same man. We'll talk about it more in a minute. Let's get out of everyone's hair for a bit."

I took a step toward the doorway. Thankfully, Cooper followed.

"Okay, but it doesn't matter what you say, Mom. I know he's the same guy."

I stood waiting for him in the doorway, but he stopped immediately when he reached Eoghanan. Spinning on his heels, Cooper faced him and pointed an accusing finger in the man's direction.

"I don't know why you're not agreeing with me, sir. I know who I saw and it was *you*." He emphasized the last word and thrust his finger forward for drama. "If you lie and say you weren't at the park *and* at the airport, I won't believe you." Switching his attitude as quickly as one could flip a switch, he spun again to face Jerry and Morna. "Thanks for the eggs. They were so yummy. See you guys later."

With that, he spun a final time, marching past me down the hall and out the front door of the inn.

"That's some lad ye have there, Grace." Jerry chuckled as he spoke.

"Yes, quite." I glanced down at my watch, drained in every imaginable way as I took off down the hallway after my son. It was only eleven a.m.

CHAPTER 6

pparently immune to jet lag, Cooper's energy didn't wane until we finally turned into the inn late that evening after hours of driving and walking around the Scottish countryside surrounding the oddly-placed inn.

I awoke the next morning much more adjusted to the time difference and determined not to be as loose-lipped or grumpy as I'd been the day before.

My resolve lasted for most of the morning. But by noon, with too little work completed, I found myself wishing for a daycare that could take Coop off my hands, if only for a few hours. He would hate every minute of it, but unless he wanted me fired, I thought it a form of torture he could handle for an afternoon—not that there was any daycare nearby to subject him to, anyway.

"Coop, if you jump up in front of my camera lens while I'm taking a photo one more time, I am going to unleash the tickle monster."

"Okay...okay. I'll stop." He collapsed onto the lawn in front of me, busying himself by picking at blades of grass. While most children would've antagonized further at the threat of a good tickle, Cooper hated it, and I knew the threat would stop him.

As if in answer to my silent prayer, Cooper jumped up in exclamation at our two approaching visitors, Jerry and Eoghanan. "Look, Mom! Look!"

Placing my camera back in its bag, I waved them over, happy to see anyone who would provide Cooper a moment of distraction.

"We come with strict instructions to see the two of ye properly fed." Eoghanan lifted the basket he held in his hands, setting it on the ground as he neared us.

"Oh, thank goodness. I'm starving." Cooper ran toward them, squeezing in between them and grabbing each man's hand as he bounced up and down.

I shook my head as I moved to greet them. "Starving? I'm sure glad I packed those gummy bears before we left. You just ate a pound of them."

Once Jerry and Eoghanan stopped walking, Cooper released their hands and stepped toward me. "I would've eaten two pounds if you'd let me."

"I have no doubt. That's why I stopped you." Though thin now, I'd been a chunky kid. I didn't wish Cooper to repeat my history.

"What is a 'gummy bear'?" Eoghanan's face twisted with confusion.

I could only hope they called them by a different name in Scotland. Surely, he knew about gummy bears if he lived on this planet.

"What? You've never had one? Well, I'll give you one right now." Cooper started to tug on the bag hanging from my shoulder. I relented, reaching inside for the bag of gummies. Once he had them in hand, he extended them to Eoghanan. "You have to try this."

After examining the candy closely, Eoghanan obliged and popped the gummy in his mouth. Watching him struggle with the texture, I couldn't help but believe he'd never tried one before.

Swallowing with effort, Eoghanan looked down at Cooper. "That is...well, that's quite an interesting food, lad."

Cooper nodded, taking his words as confirmation of the candy's deliciousness. "Yeah, I know. They're amazing."

"Thank ye for allowing me one." Eoghanan looked away from Cooper and up at me. "Could I speak with ye alone a moment, Grace?"

His question surprised me, but I nodded and nudged Cooper toward Jerry. "Coop, help Jerry spread out the blanket and get the food ready, okay?"

"Got it." He smiled over his shoulder as Eoghanan took off in the other direction.

As we walked, I rolled the top of the bag of gummies closed and started to place them back in my bag before nudging Eoghanan slightly with my elbow, waving the bag in his direction. "Would you like another?" I laughed quietly, knowing his answer even before he spoke.

"Thank ye, but no. I dinna much care for it."

I laughed while placing them back in my bag. "I could tell. Have you really never had them before? Where did you grow up?"

I thought I saw him shift uncomfortably at my question. "No, 'twas my first and last gummy bear. I grew up verra far from here, ye wouldna have heard of it."

He said nothing else, and I didn't press him but stopped walking now that we were far enough away that Cooper and Jerry couldn't hear us. "What did you want to talk to me about?"

Eoghanan stopped and faced me. "I wished to apologize for upsetting yer son yesterday morn."

"Oh, don't." I reached my hand out, placing it on the side of his arm to silence him. "It's not your fault. He only...he thought you were someone else. Really, you didn't upset him." His face turned suddenly very white. I jerked my hand away, realizing that I'd placed it right along his scar. "I'm so sorry."

He rolled his shoulder a bit in an effort to shake away the

pain. "'Tis nothing, lass. Doona worry yerself over it. I wish to ask ye if ye will allow young Cooper to join Jerry and myself this afternoon. We intend to go fishing."

His thoughtfulness in asking me away from Cooper in case I said no meant a great deal to me. He didn't wish to get Cooper's hopes up if I wouldn't allow it and didn't want to place me in an uncomfortable situation by forcing my hand. It was the act of a gentleman, and he instantly gained my trust by doing so.

"Honestly, it would be great to have a few hours of uninterrupted work. If Cooper wants to go, I have no problem with it as long as you stay near the inn and you take care of my son."

"Aye, I suspected ye might need time alone to tend to yer work." He took one step in the direction from which we'd come, indicating that we could begin our walk back.

As I moved next to him, he placed a hand on the small of my back and leaned in close. The gesture seemed slightly intimate, but I was oddly comfortable with him, and I didn't move away.

"And I promise ye, Grace," he said, "I'll return Cooper safely back to ye."

Eoghanan was still very much a stranger to me, but I believed him. He didn't seem like the type of man who would say anything he didn't mean. "I know," I muttered as we neared Jerry and Coop and moved away from one another.

"Ye are verra talented at catching the wee fish, Cooper." Eoghanan pulled the fish off its hook, tossing it back into the water to freedom.

"Yep, but I been fishin' a long time." Cooper patted him comfortingly on the shoulder. "You'll get the hang of it. Just takes practice."

Eoghanan laughed, placing another piece of bait on the hook

so Cooper could cast it into the water once again. "No, lad, I doona think my fishing will improve. The wee beasties doona like me. Who taught ye to fish?"

"My BeBop."

"What is a BeBop?" Eoghanan found the names in this century no stranger than his own.

"That's my grandfather's name. Hey, do you want a gummy? You look kinda tired or something. I think I have two more left in my pocket."

The thought of another tiny yellow or blue creature entering his mouth made Eoghanan swallow hard to wash away the lingering taste from the prior one he'd eaten. "I am tired, but why doona ye eat both of them? I doona think I'm verra hungry just now."

Cooper waved the two bears in front of him. "You sure?"

"Aye, I'm verra sure."

Smiling, the child dusted off a piece of lint from one of the gummies that had been in his pocket before he popped them both into his mouth, closing his eyes as he chewed.

Watching Cooper enjoy his mouthful, Eoghanan stood and walked over to Jerry who lay napping in the sun.

"Jerry, I think it best we make our way back. I need to do a travel with Morna, and I'd like to be back before the evening meal."

"Huh?" The old man jerked awake, his back cracking as he sat up. "What did ye say, lad?"

"I'm sorry, I dinna wish to wake ye. 'Tis only I think we should go so that I can do my travel with Morna."

"Ah, you are right." Jerry held his hand out for assistance. "Ye must help me up, though, or I'll be here all night. I doona have the same knees I once did."

"Up ye go."

He reached toward the old man with his left hand, being sure not to strain the other half of his body too much as he lifted him. Seeing Jerry to his feet, he hollered after Cooper.

"Have ye had yer fill of fishing? If so, I think it's time to go. Yer mother shall be back at the inn soon enough."

Mention of the boy's mother had Cooper gathering up his rod and tools as quickly as his little arms could move to reach them. While Eoghanan knew the boy had enjoyed their afternoon, he didn't wish to be away from his mother for too long. He didn't blame Cooper in the slightest. He found himself ready to be in Grace's presence once again, as well.

"I know we must make a journey daily, but do ye mind making it a verra short one? I wish to be back before Grace returns from her work."

"Oh, do ye now?" Morna's eyes sparkled. "I expected ye to say as much. Aye, verra short. Now, lay back so that I may begin."

He did as Morna asked, placing his left hand behind his head to prop himself up a little as she began her spell. As always, his head began to split first, the pain shooting down his spine and shaking him all over. Vision blurred quickly, but just before he evaporated entirely, he caught movement in the doorway and directed his focus just long enough to see Cooper peering inside with wide eyes.

CHAPTER 7

"Oh. My. Jiminy. Cricket. That is sooo much cooler than a spaceship! It's magic, huh? You used magic on him. Where did he go?"

Cooper's voice filled the room, and Eoghanan struggled against the fog consuming his brain to stay present. He no longer wished to make a travel today, not now that the boy had seen him. Why wouldn't Morna cease her spell? She saw the boy but continued her low chant, sending him further into oblivion.

Speech eluded him. He couldn't answer Cooper with his physical body already gone from the room. Only his hearing and sight remained, although his vision was blurred. He could hear Cooper's voice calling after Morna, but he couldn't see the room clearly, only making out the faint edges of the young lad and the witch.

Morna's voice became louder. His consciousness weakened. He couldn't be certain, but her words seemed to change, becoming different from the ones she usually spoke. Suddenly, everything went black.

47

*I*n the next instant, he was back in the room, his eyelids fluttering open to find Cooper sitting on the bed next to him, his little hands cupping both sides of his cheeks.

"Wake up, sleepy. I knew it, E-o. I knew you were the same person that was in the park and at the airport. You're magic!"

Eoghanan's head throbbed even worse than usual, but he pushed the pain aside, attributing it to the fact that his journey had been interrupted. He couldn't tell how long he'd been out, but he'd not arrived anywhere in the past. He had simply remained in the space between present and past until Morna called him back.

Eoghanan propped himself up in the bed as Cooper released hold of his face. Looking around the room for Morna, he asked, "How long was I gone?"

The witch made her way to him, extending a cool cloth to press along his forehead. "Ach, no more than a few minutes. The second the lad walked into the room, I started the return spell. I'm only pleased that all of ye arrived back here."

"Ye dinna know if I would?" The notion unsettled him. The travels were frightening enough without worrying about the possibility of his legs ending up in one century and his head in another.

"No, I couldna know for sure. This has never happened before."

"Did ye tell him?" Eoghanan glanced over at Cooper who nodded emphatically at his question.

"Yes, she did. I know everything. She's a witch and you're from, like, a million years ago. It's awesome!"

Morna shut the door to the bedroom so the three of them could speak more freely. "Aye, I dinna have a choice. I doona believe he would have ever silenced if I hadna done so. But ye needn't worry, I shall make him forget it. I was just waiting for you to wake up first."

"No way." Cooper kept his voice calm. Reaching out, he latched on hard to Eoghanan's hand. "Don't you let her put those witchy hands on me, E-o. I won't tell anybody. I promise."

Morna laughed in response, flicking her wrist in dismissal. "Doona worry, lad. I willna place a hand on ye. I'm no bad witch, surely ye can see that. I'll just say a few words, and ye willna know that ye are missing the memory."

"No." Eoghanan spoke, settling the matter in his mind. He trusted Morna completely, but it didn't mean he wished her to use magic on the lad. If knowing that magic truly existed in the world would bring the boy joy, he didn't wish to take it from him.

"Ye know we doona have a choice, Eoghanan." Morna reached to take the cloth from him, then crossed the room to hang it over the basin.

"Aye, we do. Ye have told me yerself that too few people know of the existence of magic in this present world. Now that the lad knows, doona rob him of it. I believe we can trust him. Why doona ye give Cooper and me a moment alone?"

Morna eyed him speculatively, one eyebrow raised high as she relented. "Aye, I willna spell him if ye doona wish me to. 'Tis yer secret, I suppose."

Eoghanan waited until she'd shut the door behind her to shift toward Cooper. "Now, if we doona wish for Morna to take this knowledge from ye, ye must promise me that ye willna say a word to yer mother. Such a thing is difficult for most to understand. I doona think she would believe ye."

Cooper stuck his littlest finger up by Eoghanan's nose. "I promise, promise, promise. I won't say a word to anyone."

"What is that, lad?"

"It's a pinkie promise. Haven't you ever heard of those?"

Eoghanan shook his head, "No. What is it?"

"It...um...let me show you." The boy reached for his hand, bending in his thumb and folding his first three fingers over it.

Leaving but the one smallest finger sticking out, he said, "When we wrap our pinkies together it makes the promise stick."

It made no sense to him, but Eoghanan didn't question Cooper. "Aye, 'tis our secret then. Just ye and me."

"What are you so smiley about?" I flipped the blanket and sheets back just far enough on the bed so both Cooper and I could crawl in. I climbed in first, then patted the top of the bed for him to join me.

"I had the best day ever, Mom." Clad in his dinosaur pajamas, he hopped onto the bed but didn't slip beneath the covers, instead sitting atop the comforter with his feet near my head so he could face me.

"Ever? I didn't know you were such an enthusiastic fisherman, Coop." Placing both my hands behind my head, I settled in for a bit of conversation before sleep.

"I fish with BeBop all the time and I like it, but it wasn't the fishin'."

He had both hands extended back behind him to rest his head upon, mimicking my pose, and his feet swayed back and forth.

"Well, what made it the 'best day ever,' then?"

"I can't tell you."

I rolled over on my side, smiling to the wall as I reached to turn off the lamp. "Oh, okay. Well, goodnight then, Coop. Love you."

Just as I put my finger on the lamp's knob, Cooper pounced on me. "No, Mom! Gimme a break. You know I wasn't through talking."

Laughing, I released my grip, rolling onto my back once more. "What is there to say if you won't tell me?"

He jumped from his current position and flipped himself over so that he lay on his stomach and rested his chin in the palm of his hands. "It's not that I don't want to tell you. I can't. It's a secret."

Now he had my attention.

"Now, Coop, is this a secret someone told you, or one you learned by spying? Because those are two very different things, and we've already talked about this before—it's not okay to eavesdrop on people."

I watched him wrestle with my question, his face contorting as he lifted his brow and shifted his lower lip in between his teeth. As always, he didn't want to lie, but he knew I wouldn't like the truth, either.

Rolling off the edge of the bed, he silently walked over to my side, reaching up on his tiptoes to turn off the light. Enveloped in darkness, he crawled over me and onto the bed, slipping under the sheets on his side again.

"I just got real sleepy, Mom. Goodnight. Angels on your pillow."

I rolled my eyes in the darkness, leaning over to kiss him on the forehead. "Angels on yours too, Coop. It was a little bit of both, huh?"

Silence followed my question for a minute or two, and then his voice, soft and sweet in its confession, answered. "Yep, maybe a little."

I woke early, hoping to get a jump on looking through all the photographs I'd taken the day before, and perhaps get a little writing done on the article, too. Coop always rose early, so it came as no surprise to find his half of the bed empty.

When he outgrew his crib several years ago, I moved him into his own room with a "big boy" bed. I made it my goal to figure out just what time he awoke each morning by setting my alarm at a different time each day—continually setting it earlier and earlier if I woke to find him already up. It didn't matter what time I set it, Coop's internal clock was determined to beat the alarm. I would walk into his room every morning to find him playing with his toys. Eventually, I'd given up the effort and settled for rising by six each morning so that, even if he woke earlier, he wouldn't be unsupervised for very long.

I knew he wouldn't have gone far and suspected he'd made his way downstairs to the kitchen, hoping to lend a helping hand with the breakfast preparations. Still, Cooper's idea of helping wasn't always viewed the same way by others. Deciding to forgo a shower for the moment, I brushed my hair and teeth, pulled on a pair of jeans and a t-shirt, and left in search of my son.

I heard him before I saw him, giggling at the deep Scottish voice making a gurgled, horrible sound that I could only assume was an attempt at a dinosaur noise. Sure enough, as I descended the stairs I saw Eoghanan sprawled out on his left side next to Cooper on the floor of the living room.

Each held a dinosaur—Cooper a small one with wings, Eoghanan a large T-Rex. While Cooper had the advantage by keeping his dinosaur in the air, Eoghanan had his creature jumping to unimaginable heights for the short stubbiness of the dinosaur's legs. It sent Cooper into a fit of laughter each time.

"You're cheating." He said it smiling, not bothered by Eoghanan's imaginative dinosaur play. "That dinosaur couldn't jump like that."

"How do ye know that? Have ye seen a dinosaur?"

By this point I'd reached the bottom of the stairs, but I stayed where they couldn't see me for a moment, not wishing to interrupt their conversation. Perhaps I knew where my son's penchant for eavesdropping came from, after all.

"No. Have *you*?"Cooper asked the question with such genuine curiosity that it left me baffled. Of course Eoghanan had never seen a dinosaur, and Cooper knew it.

"No, lad. I havena traveled that far back. Not at all."

For the life of me, I couldn't begin to imagine what they were talking about. Out of the loop, and frustrated with my lack of understanding at their conversation, I decided to make my presence known.

"Good morning. Please tell me that you were awake when Coop found you." I looked sympathetically at Eoghanan as I neared, sitting down on the edge of the couch next to them.

"Aye, I was. I doona sleep verra much." Eoghanan shifted so that he could stand from his place on the floor, looking rather pleased with himself as he did so. "Ah, it feels nice to be able to move more freely. That dinna hurt me at all."

"Good, I'm so glad." I placed my hand on his back in a sort of congratulations. The warmth that shot through my fingers at the touch sent a jolt through my body. I enjoyed the unfamiliar feeling, but I felt him shiver a bit beneath my hand, and I jerked away awkwardly, worried that I'd made him uncomfortable. I had a tendency to be that way with people—to touch them in comfort or understanding. I supposed it was the mom in me.

Quickly, I bent to lift Cooper up into my arms to break the tension. After a good long hug, he pulled away, jerking his head toward the kitchen.

"Morna asked if I wanted to go work some sheep today."

I smiled at his statement, not sure if I was more pleased at how excited he seemed over some sheep or at the prospect of having at least part of the day to look through my photos and write without his assistance.

"Sheep, huh? Do you want to go?"

He thought my question ridiculous. I could tell from how his eyes bulged when I asked it, and he twisted free so he could grab my hand and pull me back toward the staircase.

"Of course I want to go! I need to go put on some sheep working clothes, Mom. Let's go."

For such a small kid, he did a fair job of pulling me across the floor. Shaking his hand free, I waved him ahead of me. "Go on, Coop. I'm right behind you."

Rubbing the sleep from my eyes, I trudged up the stairs after him, watching as he stripped off his pajama top even before reaching the bedroom door.

CHAPTER 9

I worked consistently throughout the morning, zoned in to the screen of my laptop, clicking through photos and sporadically trying to get a start on the article. After the growl of my stomach became too loud to ignore, I finally decided to take a break.

As I made my way down the hallway, I created a mental task list, running through all of the places still left to explore and photograph, hoping I could remember them long enough to write them all down after grabbing a bite to eat. Midway down my mental list, I passed the last door before the staircase and a deep scream inside Eoghanan's room made me shriek. I jumped as high as Cooper's T-Rex.

"Grace?" Eoghanan's voice from somewhere inside the room calmed me immediately. I'd not realized that he'd stayed behind.

The door was cracked slightly, and I stepped forward to push it open, one hand on my rapidly beating heart. I didn't find him in the main room, but I could hear him grumbling something from inside the bathroom and moved toward the sound of his voice.

"Eoghanan, are you okay? Why did you scream?"

I stepped into the center of the room and saw that the bathroom door was ajar.

Hearing movement from inside, I turned away before glimpsing him, but still felt like I'd invaded his privacy. "Oh…gosh. So sorry." My bare toe caught the corner of the bed, sending me sprawling onto the floor, arms and legs spread wide.

"Are ye hurt, lass?" Eoghanan asked, his voice in the room now.

"I'm fine," I said, remaining on the floor, folding in one arm to shield my eyes in case he'd rushed out of the bathroom undressed.

He laughed, and I could imagine his body shaking from the effort of it. "Forgive me. 'Tis not that ye fell that amuses me, but 'twas quite the sight. Allow me to help ye stand."

I held up my other hand to stop him. "Wait. Do you need to get a towel or something?"

"All is well, lass."

With the only injured party being my big toe, I stood and turned, colliding abruptly with Eoghanan's broad chest. Thank goodness he was fully dressed, but I'd not been on a date since before Cooper's birth, and the contact stirred something inside me that I'd almost forgotten ever feeling—a strong attraction to someone of the opposite sex.

"What was yer name again, lass? I doona think it can be Grace. 'Tis not verra fitting."

I laughed. He couldn't be more right about that. "Yeah, it never has been very fitting. Why did you scream?"

Reluctantly, I lifted my gaze away from his broad chest to his face, surprised by his embarrassed expression.

"I dinna scream. I doona scream, lass."

I rolled my eyes—typical man. "That was a scream if I've ever heard one."

"No." He released me. Reaching up, he thumbed my nose gently. The gesture was playful, and I smiled as he moved back toward the bathroom. "Will ye help me with these beastly..." he hesitated. "Ye call them knobs, aye?"

I nodded, my brows pulled in. He baffled me. How could a grown man, seemingly containing all his mental faculties, know so little about the simplest things?

Apparently, I needn't say anything for him to see how odd I thought the question. "I told ye, lass," he explained, "I dinna grow up amongst such things as these. I nearly melted the skin off my hand trying to start the water."

So, that explained the scream. "All right." I stepped into the cramped bathroom with him, reaching down past him to fiddle with the shower knobs. "Just exactly where did you grow up? I'm starting to imagine you being raised by monkeys and swinging from the trees." I laughed. He certainly had the physique of *Tarzan*.

Eoghanan shook his head, testing the water temperature with his fingers. "No, I doona think I've ever seen a monkey." He smiled. "Thank ye, the water feels much better."

"Good. I'll leave you to it then." I stepped from the room, pausing just outside the door when my grumbling stomach reminded me of my manners. "Have you eaten anything? I thought I'd go round up something for myself. I'll bring you up something, too, if you'd like."

He nodded. "Aye, I'd love that, lass."

His smiled widened, and my heart literally fluttered in my chest. Taking a breath to regain some sense of composure, I went down to the kitchen.

* * *

I spent the entire length of our salted-cracker lunch apologizing at regular intervals for our lack of food choices. "You're going to be starving by dinner. I truly am sorry. It's as if Morna uses magic to cook her meals. Seriously, I don't understand it. She's always cooking, but she has nothing in her cupboards. It's astonishing."

"Grace . . . " Eoghanan reached out and squeezed my hand, holding it long enough to quicken my pulse. "If ye apologize once more, I willna eat another bite. 'Tis not yer job, nor Morna's, to see me fed." Winking, he popped another cracker into his mouth.

I watched him eat, observing him closely. He lifted every cracker with his left hand, leaving his right arm hanging at his side. He did such a good job of compensating with his left arm that I'd not noticed how little he used his right. Still, something about the way he gripped things seemed a little unnatural, and I ventured a guess that he was actually right-handed. "You write with your right hand, don't you?"

The left corner of his mouth lifted as he shifted to face me. "Aye. Fortunately, I remain able to do so as long as I doona move my elbow too much. When the sword came down, it cut me deepest right along my shoulder muscle." He paused, lifting his left hand as he traced one of his fingers along his shoulder, showing me the path of his injury. "It hit my bone and turned, traveling underneath and along my ribs. 'Tis made my right shoulder difficult to move, but Morna says it will eventually heal."

I sensed my eyes widening until it felt as if they would pop out of my head. Whatever I'd imagined as the cause of his injuries, I'd not considered a blade—a piece of machinery perhaps, but not a weapon. "A sword?"

"Aye, a mighty large one." He took a long look at my face, observing my shocked expression. "Doona worry, lass. He's dead now—the man who did this to me."

He said it so dismissively that I couldn't help swallowing a laugh. It wasn't the condition of his assailant that worried me, as he seemed to think. I was more concerned with knowing why someone had come at Eoghanan with a sword, of all things.

Just as I opened my mouth to ask, he changed the conversation entirely.

"I'm sorry if I frightened ye. Ye thought yerself alone, aye?"

"Yes, I did, but there's no need to apologize."

He nodded and blew a long strand of unruly hair out of his face. It was a habitual action on his part, and I wondered if months of being unable to lift his right shoulder had left him feeling less groomed than he was accustomed to being.

"Would you..." I hesitated, hoping I wasn't about to overstep the boundaries of propriety. "Would you like me to cut your hair for you?" I pointed to the curly strand that kept falling across his face. "You sometimes act as if it's in your way." When he didn't answer immediately, I added, "Or I could at least pull it back for you?"

He glanced up toward his forehead, his eyes crossing as he made eye contact with the annoying strand. "If ye doona mind. I wouldna wish to take ye from yer work."

"Ah . . . " I waved a hand dismissively. "I'm finished for now. This seems more urgent." I reached both hands up toward his head. "May I?" He nodded, and I slipped my fingers into his red locks, messing his hair around to get a feel for how it needed to be cut.

I'd cut Cooper's hair his entire life, and although the shade of Eoghanan's was different, the texture was very much the same as my son's—curly and not easily tamed, bouncing out of place on a whim, or so it seemed. Eoghanan's neck relaxed as I played with his hair, and his eyes closed in pleasure. It occurred to me that men didn't often experience the lovely feeling of having someone play with their hair.

He sighed. "If ye insist on doing this, I doona have it in me to argue."

"I do insist. You'll feel much better when you get rid of some of this." I stood and moved behind him, lifting the hair at the base of his neck. He tilted his head back into my hands and I massaged his scalp as I gathered the strands. "Do you always keep your hair long?"

"Hmm...?"

I looked down at his face from above him, and he smiled as his eyes flickered open.

"What did ye ask me, Grace? By God, that feels nice."

"Yes, a good head massage always does. I asked if you always keep your hair long."

"Oh, aye, but do what ye wish with it. I doona much care."

His eyes closed again, and I laughed, tugging on a strand at the base of his neck. "Hey, don't fall asleep on me. It'll be hard for me to cut your hair that way."

He reached his left hand up and grabbed my fingers, bringing them to rest in his hand and on his shoulder, "Oh, doona ye worry, I am verra, verra awake. 'Twould be impossible for me to sleep with yer hands on me."

I pulled away, glad that his eyes were closed so he couldn't see the blush on my face. "Stand up and let's move your chair into the bathroom. I don't want to trim your hair over the carpet."

He did as I asked. Once he was vertical, I dragged his chair across to the tile floor, surprised to find a pair of scissors resting in a small basket on the bathroom sink, and wrapping cloths, washcloths, and a large jar of a homemade salve, as well. "What's all this?" I asked as Eoghanan joined me. He sat down in the chair and slipped his shirt off, then leaned his head back into my open hands.

"The salve? 'Tis what Morna applies to my wound each day. Makes it herself."

"Up you go." I lifted his head and turned on the faucet, dousing my hands so I could run them through his hair, re-wetting the strands so I could comb them through. "Has Morna treated your wound today?"

"No. I shall do it myself once ye have finished."

I examined his scar as I combed his hair. It would be a messy job if he tried to apply the salve himself, and I imagined it wouldn't feel good on his shoulder. "No, I'll do it when I'm finished with your hair."

"There's no need. I doona wish to worry ye with such a gruesome chore."

As my gaze traveled over his bare torso, 'gruesome' was not a word that entered my mind. Yes, the wound had a wicked appearance, but he was still a gorgeous man.

"Poor Morna," he continued. "She often winces when she tends to the wound, as if the sight of me hurts her eyes."

With his hair sufficiently wet and combed, I picked up the scissors and set to work, one curl at a time. "It doesn't hurt my eyes to look at you. Quite the opposite actually."

I hadn't meant to voice my thoughts, and there was no hiding the heat that spread up my neck—not this time—not with him staring up at me from the mirror. I flinched inside. What was it about this man that made me blurt out whatever crossed my mind?

I glanced up to see both corners of his mouth quirk a bit, as if trying to hold back a smile. But as soon as he caught my attention, he let it loose. "Aye? Is that so, lass?" He twisted in his chair to look at me.

Deciding there was no way to answer without further embarrassing myself, I placed my hands on either side of his head and twisted him back around to the front. "Unless you want to end up bald, I suggest you quit squirming in your seat."

He laughed loudly but obeyed, stiffening his shoulder as he sat up straight. "As ye wish, lass. As ye wish."

CHAPTER 10

*E*oghanan woke the next morning energized in a way unfamiliar to him. Lying with his eyes still closed, he reveled in it—the newness of the feeling of a good night's sleep. Instead of awaking on edge, his jaw clenched and shoulders tight, he experienced a pleasant numbness radiating down his body. His shoulders were loose, his mouth still open wide from sleeping so deeply. He usually never slept more than a few brief moments at a time each night, waking often and with his mind churning.

It had not always been the case. As a young boy, still free and naïve of life's inevitable woes, he'd been able to sleep until the sun was far into the sky each day. When Osla – his brother's first wife – had died, everything changed for Eoghanan. Unable to save her, an impenetrable sense of failure and guilt settled over him. Impenetrable, until now.

While the blade Niall had run down his body nearly killed him, it had also saved Eoghanan in ways he was just beginning to understand. Without such an injury, he would never have journeyed to this strange time. He would never have met Grace.

Her presence here was no accident, of that he was now certain. Morna had lied to him when she'd said she didn't control where he went on his travels. She was too much of a matchmaker, and Grace's arrival at the small inn was too odd to be a coincidence. The old witch had shown him the lass for a reason. Eoghanan couldn't help but hope that him meeting Grace was meant to fill some missing piece of his soul.

For over seven years, he'd shut out any possibility of love for another woman, paying a silent penance for sins that weren't his own. Now that his brother, Baodan, knew the truth and his burden had been lifted, he was free to start his life anew. Free to become the man he'd once been, a man filled with passion, desire, and love—all of the things he'd denied himself for far too many years.

With his eyes still closed, he listened to Grace's voice near him and smiled. She stood outside his door, chattering so quickly he couldn't understand a word she said. He was content to simply listen to the rhythm of her voice.

Just thinking of her pushed away any remnant of sleepiness that remained. He couldn't remember the last time a lass had stirred his blood so, and he was certain she felt the same about him. Whether she'd intended to or not, she'd all but admitted as much to him.

As he shifted his feet over the side of the bed to stand, he suddenly recognized the sound of his name amongst Grace's quickly-spoken words. Moving silently across the floor, he pressed his ear against the door, curious to hear what she said about him.

"What?" Grace said, sounding shocked.

Eoghanan waited for an answer from the person with whom she spoke, but the silence stretched on. He then realized she must be speaking into a telephone—that odd contraption Morna had spent the better half of an hour trying to explain to him, with little success. He couldn't understand the need to reach someone so immediately, unless to bring news of a death or a threat. Still, he pressed his ear closer, hoping to learn enough from Grace's side of the conversation to gain its meaning.

"What?" I laughed more from shock than from thinking my sister funny. Her question could not be a serious one.

Jane snorted. "You heard what I said. Do you have a thing for this guy?"

"A *thing*? Just what is that supposed to mean, and why would you even wonder it?"

"Goodness, it is so easy to get a rise out of you, Grace." Jane laughed loudly into the phone, and I could imagine her delighted smile.

"All I said was that there was someone else staying at the inn with me and Cooper. He..." I stuttered. It only made sense that Jane would come to the conclusion that something was going on between Eoghanan and me. Why else would I bring him up? It's not as if it was unusual for operating inns to have more than one guest at a time. I'd simply found myself wanting to talk about him, to discuss him with someone who wasn't five years old. "He seems very nice, is all. Cooper really likes him."

"Hmm..." Jane waited a moment, presumably hoping I would say more. When I didn't, she continued. "Cooper likes him, huh? Are you sure it isn't *Grace* that likes him?"

I smiled, thinking of Eoghanan and me sharing lunch in his room. His glorious accent. The way he often winked at me as he spoke. His heart-stopping smile. And then, after lunch, the way he'd looked without his shirt . . . "Maybe it's not *just* Cooper that likes him. I like him, too. So what? Is that really such a big deal, Jane?"

The guffaw-ey gasp that came from the other end of the phone made me immediately regret my admission. "Maybe it is a big deal. It sure sounds to me as if you've got it bad for this guy. I'm not saying there's anything wrong with that. In fact, I'm glad."

A sudden thump against Eoghanan's door caused me to

murmur a quick, "Hang on just a sec," before throwing the phone down next to its base. I cautiously rested an ear against Eoghanan's door, listening for any movement. Obviously, he still slept. If he'd been up, I knew there was a chance he could have heard me. I was literally half a foot away from his door. Breathing a sigh of relief, I stepped away, picking up the receiver once more to continue my explanation. "Okay, okay," I said to my sister. "I admit it. Eoghanan is a-ma-zing. I've never met another man like him. Unfortunately, because of that, I'm a bumbling mess around him. He took off his shirt and I couldn't stop myself from blurting out every thought in my head." I cringed again at the thought of it.

More laughter traveled across the phone line. "So...what did he look like? Good, I'm guessing since you flipped out."

As ridiculous as it was, my knees became a bit rubbery at the memory. "He looked . . . wow. Just wow. With a capital 'W.'" My sisters were the only people who could revert me from the full-grown mother I was today to the boy-crazed teenage girl I had once been. Of all my sisters, Jane was especially talented at this feat.

"Well, then." Jane chuckled. "This is interesting. What a great story you'll have to carry back with you when you come home." She changed her voice in a very poor attempt to mimic my own. "You see, I was going to marry Jeffrey, my very best friend in the whole world, but then I came to my senses and fled the wedding. I flew to Scotland the very next day for work. While I was there, I had a wild fling with a native Scot." She dropped the mimic and went back to being Jane. "I'm serious, that's an awesome story. One to tell your grandkids one day."

I ran a hand through my hair in exasperation. "No grandkid ever wants to hear about their grandmother's wild fling, Jane. Ever. Not that we're going to have one. Eoghanan's such a gentleman. There's something about him. He's . . . I don't know, old-fashioned, I guess. But in a good way."

"Old-fashioned how? I'm not sure what you mean."

"Never mind. I'm not sure what I mean, either." Glancing at my watch, I decided it best to direct the conversation to the reason I'd called Jane so I could get back to work. "Besides, we seem to have gotten very side-tracked here. I just wanted to check in on Mom and Father. On a scale of one-to-ten, just how angry is he?"

She paused—evidently his anger ranked at a ten. "I don't know. Maybe…maybe, like, an 8.75?"

It was a very Jane answer. "8.75?"

"Yeah. I mean, he really didn't get as angry as I'd expected. When we realized you'd bailed, I thought he'd literally turn into some sort of dragon and just burn up everybody with his rage. He didn't, though. He's still human so, yeah, less angry than I expected. He's still very, very pissed, though. It was weird, like a small part of him knew you wouldn't go through with the wedding. That being said, I cannot imagine the earful Jeffrey got from him. Not the best of times to leave him to deal with Father, although I know you had to for work."

"I know, I know." I'd been trying my best not to think of what I'd left Jeffrey to deal with alone. It made my gut twist with guilt. "I really need to get back to work. I just wanted to check in on things. I love you, Jane."

"I love you too, Grace." I could envision her leaning her head tenderly into the phone's ear piece, just as she would have done to my shoulder had I been standing next to her. "I'm proud of you, ya know? We all are. Mom, me, everyone except Father, I imagine. The whole thing was ridiculous. I'm glad you didn't go through with it."

"Me, too." I couldn't express the extent of my gladness. For the first time in my entire life, I felt like I'd truly liberated myself from my father's ruling thumb. "Talk soon." I hung up the phone, determined to get at least a little work accomplished.

ry as he might, Eoghanan couldn't relax his smile. His cheeks hurt, unaccustomed to staying in the lifted position for so long. After Grace had ended her telephone conversation, he'd slumped against the wall in relief. There'd been a brief moment when Grace had almost caught him listening. They'd both had their ears pressed against either side of his door while he held his breath, hoping she wouldn't hear him.

Although he was only a party to Grace's side of the telephone conversation, she had only said good things about him. Wonderful things. She'd said that she liked him, and that Cooper did, as well. Eoghanan couldn't be more pleased to hear it. He very much liked the wee lad, and he liked the boy's mother even more.

She'd also spoken about his bare chest. While he was not familiar with the word she'd used to describe his appearance, her voice held no note of displeasure. Rather, she'd said it breathlessly, with a tone of admiration. And she had called him a gentleman, which honored him, although he did not understand the word she had used to further describe him in the end. Old-fashioned. But in a "good way," she'd said. He smiled. Only one thing gave Eoghanan pause—the absence of Cooper's father. He assumed the man must be dead, but couldn't be certain.

Rested and fully alive, Eoghanan peeked into the hallway. Finding it empty, he went in search of Jerry. He wished to ask Grace to do something special with him, but he needed advice on what the times called for and to find assurance that Grace was free to be pursued.

He found Jerry in back of the inn, tending to a small garden with Morna.

"Ach, there ye are, lad. Morna and I have something to ask ye."

Eoghanan lifted a brow in surprise, nodding in encouragement that they proceed.

Morna stepped toward him, placing her hand on the side of

his arm. "Jerry and I made a dinner reservation in the city a while back, but I doona think either one of us is up to it this evening. We thought perhaps ye might like to take Grace in our place."

"Reservation?"

"Aye, at a lovely place in the center of Edinburgh. I have directions, and I have something fitting for ye to wear. Why doona ye ask her? She'll say yes, I know it. Be sure to tell her that she will have to drive, though. Tell her that ye canna due to yer injured shoulder. She willna mind."

The witch could obviously read his mind, for she presented him with the very opportunity he'd wished for before he'd had the opportunity to ask how to make it happen. A special evening alone with Grace.

In the midst of his excitement, he forgot the other question he had meant to ask Jerry.

CHAPTER 11

*E*oghanan's invitation came as a surprise, albeit a lovely one. Perhaps it really wasn't too much of a surprise when I thought back on all the subtle flirtation between us the previous day. Still, it had been so long since I'd been asked out on any sort of date, I'd begun to believe that my last first date over six years ago would be my last date ever.

Eoghanan asked me to dinner in the most adorable way—knocking on the door of my bedroom and speaking to Cooper first, saying something along the lines of, "I believe Morna needs yer assistance, young Cooper. Seems she's found a snail in an unfortunate place and doesna wish to pick it up herself."

Cooper, eager to help and overly excited by anything remotely gross, leapt up from his place on the floor. "A snail? Well, I'll get it for her."

Cooper ran down the stairs quickly, leaving Eoghanan and me alone, where he shifted back and forth nervously in the doorway for a minute before speaking.

"Grace, do ye have a dress with ye here?"

I turned my head inquisitively, smiling internally at his question. It seemed an odd way to start the conversation. "Uh, yeah I do, actually. It's not all-together fancy, more of just a sundress. Why do you ask?"

"I hoped that ye might join me for dinner in Edinburgh. Would ye like to? I should tell ye that ye will have to steer the car. I doona think my shoulder will allow it."

"Edinburgh?" I couldn't help the surprise and hesitation in my voice. It wasn't like Edinburgh was just down the road. "That's over three hours away."

"Ah." He looked down at his feet a bit, embarrassed. "So 'tis no, then? 'Tis not the best idea."

"No." I moved toward him, shaking my head to stop him. "That's not what I said. I'm only a bit surprised."

"Aye."

I smiled, hoping my initial reaction hadn't disappointed him. A three-hour drive would take us away from the inn for an entire day, which appealed to me greatly. I imagined Eoghanan was in dire need of a change of scenery, as well. I doubted he'd traveled outside a ten-mile radius of the inn since arriving here. A break away might also be of benefit to my work if I could stop and take some photos along the way. "I think that sounds great. I can be ready in half an hour." I glanced over at the mirror on the wall across from me and looked sheepishly back at him. "Forty-five, tops. What about Cooper?"

"If 'tis all right with ye, Morna said she and Jerry might take him to explore Conall Castle. 'Tis just down the road a ways."

Cooper would be thrilled at the idea. "He'll love that. Meet you downstairs in a bit?"

He smiled, nodded once, and left me alone to get ready. I started stripping my clothes off as soon as the door closed, resigning myself to the fact that, once again, I would get little work done today. It was becoming a very bad habit.

"**A**re ye certain I doona look a fool? Do men not wear kilts in Scotland anymore?" Eoghanan looked down at the khaki slacks and dark blue shirt Morna had dressed him in, utterly unsure about his new outfit. The linen pants and stretchy shorts were sensible garb for lounging around the inn, for they kept pressure off his scar, but to appear in front of other people without his kilt seemed very strange to him.

"Ye look nothing like a fool. Ye look like a man every lass in the Highlands will admire. Best keep Grace on yer arm so they know ye are taken."

"Taken?" It seemed a fast conclusion for the old lass to come to, though he liked the way it sounded very much. "I barely know the lass. 'Taken' is not the right word."

Morna clucked her tongue at him dismissively. "If ye say so, though I doona know why ye would doubt a thing I say to ye. I have my way of knowing things that others do not."

He knew that better than anyone, but said nothing as he heard Grace's footsteps on the stairs. Turning, he took in the sight of her as she approached. She was a beautiful lass by any standard. Even casually dressed in her usual strange trousers that women of this time period wore, and with her long hair pulled up loosely off her neck and out of her eyes, he thought her breathtaking.

But now, dressed in a light blue dress that reached slightly past her knees, the sleeves capping just over her shoulders, Eoghanan could scarcely catch his breath. She'd let her hair down. The long blonde strands fell loosely about her shoulders.

Suddenly Morna's hand smacked him roughly against the back, reminding him to speak up like a grown man rather than the young awkward lad he suddenly felt himself to be.

"Grace. That is...well...a verra nice dress."

She laughed, and some of his nervousness lifted away. Eoghanan smiled.

"Thanks," Grace said. "You don't look so bad yourself. Nice haircut."

"Aye." He lifted his hand to touch a small spot on the back of his head, winking at her as he did so. "Only exception being this wee bit here. The lass who trimmed my hair got rather distracted for a moment."

"That's so weird," said Cooper, who Eoghanan realized stood beside his mother. Until that moment, he'd not noticed the boy with Grace.

A bit ashamed that he'd completely missed the boy, Eoghanan glanced across into Cooper's eyes. "Weird? What do ye mean, lad?"

"Mom's never messed up my hair when she cuts it." The lad made his way to Eoghanan's side. "What did you do? Tickle her?" He giggled.

Grace glanced up at Eoghanan a bit sheepishly, a pretty blush coloring her cheeks.

Reaching down, he gripped Cooper's shoulder. "Aye, yer mother did a fine job. I only spoke in jest. Are ye excited about yer trip with Morna and Jerry?"

"Oh, yes. So, so, so excited. I've never seen a real castle before. Only on TV and stuff."

Grace crossed to Cooper, then picked him up and hugged him. "I'm sure you're going to have a great time. Just promise me that you'll listen to whatever they say, Coop."

The young lad regarded her seriously. "'Course I will, Mom. I only get rowdy for you, ya know?"

Grace laughed, leaning in to kiss Cooper's forehead. "Yes, I do know. Thanks for that."

The boy laughed, squirming so she would set him down. "You're welcome."

Once Cooper retreated toward Morna and Jerry, Grace took Eoghanan's arm and whispered, "Let's get out of here."

Gladly, he turned her toward the door, his pulse racing in anticipation of spending their day together.

***

For the first half hour of our drive, Eoghanan remained unusually silent. If I'd not been watching him closely out of the corner of my eye, I would've been worried that he was less interested in me than he'd first appeared. Instead, I found that it wasn't a lack of interest in conversation with me, but a rather obvious fascination with the workings of the car that kept him silent.

He watched everything I did closely; from adjusting the mirrors to shifting the gears, he watched with wide eyes, and his mouth kept opening and closing in the same way Cooper's often did if he wanted to ask a question, but then thought better of it. I sensed an unexplainable nervousness in Eoghanan as I pushed the car to a reasonable cruising speed, though he tried to hide it.

"Do cars make you nervous?"

Eoghanan directed his attention to me fully for the first time since the beginning of the car ride. Smiling, he shook his head in a fashion that seemed more about pushing away his thoughts than in answer to my question. "No, though ye do."

"Me?" The thought that I made him nervous seemed entirely absurd to me, but the confession endeared him to me even more. He had the unique ability to simultaneously seem completely confident, yet vulnerable.

"Aye. Ye are stunning, Grace. I have never seen anyone as beautiful as ye and it...aye." He sighed loudly. "I canna help but be nervous around ye. 'Tis a verra nice feeling."

My breath caught, and I looked back at the road. I'd never met a man more honest about his feelings, or more flattering in the things he said about me. And it didn't seem like false flattery —just a way of getting on my good side.

The interior of the car suddenly seemed too small, and the attraction between us took on a life of its own. I felt his presence like a touch, the energy emanating from his body mingling with mine. It occurred to me, then, being so near to him made me nervous, too.

"You like to be nervous?" I asked, when I was able to breathe again. As a mother, I lived in a constant state of slight anxiety. I disliked nothing more than being nervous.

"Aye."

He reached over and brushed my hair back away from my shoulder—a gesture that sent a shockwave so great down my spine I had to grip the wheel to keep from swerving off the road.

"Nerves, as ye call them, remind me that I can feel something other than regret and worry," he said, his voice a deep and gentle caress. "I havena felt that way about much of anything in a verra long time."

"Oh." I hardly knew what to say in response. It pained me to think that he'd lived with such pain. But he was also clear that I made him feel differently, which was the headiest of compliments. "We can talk about it, if you'd like to. Your regrets and worries, I mean. But only if you want to. It's just . . . I've been there, you know? I *am* there. Every day. Sometimes it seems as if I'm in a constant state of worry about Cooper and if I'm being a good enough mother to him. And my regrets—well, that's a whole other story." I blurted a short laugh. "I guess what I'm trying to say is, I can relate. And I wouldn't judge."

"Thank ye, lass. But I doona want to think about that sort of thing. Not today." He trailed his hand from my shoulder down to cover my free hand where it rested on my thigh. "But I would like to say that, just in the short time I've known ye, I'm as certain as I've ever been of anything that ye are a good mother to Cooper. The two of ye together warms the heart."

"Thank you. I hope so. For you to say it means a lot to me. I try to do my best with him. He's a joy." I laughed again. "Well, most of the time."

The car grew silent again. I felt a fluttering in my heart. Nothing unusual. I felt it anytime I was near him, but in the confines of the car it seemed more intense—like a hum of happy energy so strong it vibrated. The sensation was thrilling and unsettling at the same time. Eyeballs deep in mommy-world since Cooper's birth, I'd gone far too long without the affection of a man. And most of the men I'd been with before had not had the most honorable intentions when it came to our relationship. But Eoghanan was a gentleman if I'd ever seen one. Simply from the look in his eyes, I knew without a doubt that he couldn't tell a lie if he tried. And he actually seemed to like me as much as I did him. No man had ever stirred such feelings in me as he did, and for some reason, it scared me.

Suddenly I had the strongest urge to escape those feelings before they overwhelmed me and I did or said something stupid. Because a second urge had risen up in me, one in conflict with my need to escape. I wanted to throw caution to the wind and kiss him. I wanted it so much. Too much, maybe.

Just another reason that escape seemed the safest urge to follow through on.

Glancing out the side window, I spotted a hill scattered with flowers. While pretty enough, it wasn't out of the ordinary, but like a dozen other flower-dotted hills in the country. Still, I pulled the car over, desperate to put some space between us.

I needed to think, to make sense of what was happening to me.

CHAPTER 12

If Eoghanan thought my abrupt stop to admire the flowers odd, he didn't show it. I wondered if he felt the same stirring need to kiss me as I did him and welcomed the chance to put some distance between us that the confines of the car didn't allow, if only for a few minutes.

After returning to the car and continuing the journey into Edinburgh, he made a pointed effort to engage in conversation. At least while we listened and responded to one another, our minds weren't left to daydream about crossing the line into something beyond friendship. I found his old-fashioned reserve refreshing. So few men of my generation—and women, for that matter—took things slowly when it came to romance, which often led to regret. Eoghanan seemed to respect my heart.

Throughout dinner, we managed to keep the conversation going, though it consisted of mainly pointless jabber. We discussed my work, Scotland, the inn, Morna and Jerry, but nothing very personal. An unspoken understanding had developed between us—anything personal that might evoke emotion would put us in that place again—a place neither of us took lightly, having both been wounded by love in the past. Although he'd said nothing of the sort, and it seemed hard to believe by looking at him, I got the feeling that perhaps Eoghanan was just as 'out of the game' as I was. Just as unfamiliar with what was expected on a date. Just as silently eager for a human connection, yet wary of it at the same time.

When we finished eating and he had paid our bill, a strained silence fell over us once again, but this time I made no effort to end it, exhausted from hours of forced conversation. I couldn't help but be a little disappointed, only because I knew this date wasn't a fair representation of how we could be together. Though we'd not spoken too much, we'd only known each other a few days. And, actually, conversation flowed more naturally with Eoghanan than with anyone I had ever met before. It was true that he scared me, or more accurately, the way he made me feel scared me, and I'd allowed my fear to dictate our conversation. I expected he'd done the same, and we rode most of the way back to the inn silently and, I suspected, mutually feeling as if we'd let one another down. Not to mention ourselves.

Finally, less than a mile away from the inn, Eoghanan reached over to squeeze my hand. "That was rotten, lass. I doona wish to discuss the weather nor the countryside with ye. 'Tis not why I asked ye to come here, not to speak to ye as I would a stranger. I know I havena known ye but a few days, but it doesna feel that way. Not to me. I doona believe it does to ye, either. I wish to know everything about ye, about what ye did as a child, about yer family. I want ye to tell me what ye want out of yer life and for wee Cooper's life, as well. And I wish to tell ye about myself. I want to speak to ye about things that matter, but I canna do that just yet."

"Why not?" It was the only thing I could force myself to say in response to him. He gave the perfect speech—exactly what every woman wants to hear. A man wanting to actually learn more about her...by means of communication. Every man I'd ever known had found meaningful conversation extremely challenging. Was Eoghanan the exception?

I don't think I would've believed such an exclamation from just anyone, but I knew that he told the truth. He was different; I sensed it the first moment I saw him. He didn't play games, didn't pretend to be someone he wasn't.

It took him a moment to answer. I could sense his hesitation in the way he gripped my hand. He kept squeezing it, releasing it, squeezing it again, all the while running his thumb back and forth over the top of my knuckles.

"Because..."

He exhaled loudly, and I slipped my thumb from his grasp, bringing it around to stroke the top of his hand, hoping to comfort him. My mommy-gene, my inherent need to soothe, had come through once again.

"Lass, if ye told me those things just now, all of the important details about ye, I wouldna hear them. I can think of nothing other than what yer hair would feel like if I ran my fingers through it, how yer lips would feel against my own. So please, continue to speak to me about the weather and yer boss, Mr. Perdie, but remember that I do wish to hear everything else. I just canna hear it right now, not when I'm so bewitched by ye."

My heart beat in quick time, and I had to hold my breath because I knew it would come out shaky. I replayed his words in my head again and again. Each time, they sounded more swoon-worthy than the last. I said nothing, only slowly pressed down on the brake and pulled the car to the side of the road.

I realized that Eoghanan mistook my response as soon as I threw the car into park and unbuckled my seatbelt.

"Ach, I've behaved as a fool, Grace," he said. "Forgive me. I dinna mean any disrespect to ye. My words were meant as a compliment. I dinna wish for ye to think that I was bored with ye. I know the conversation may have seemed that way. I'm sorry.

Truly. I doona know...I am not verra good at speaking with women."

"Hush." I was certain my eyes were hazy with longing. It had been so long since I'd felt such a need, I scarcely knew how to handle the emotion. Trembling, I placed one finger on his lips just long enough to silence him, and then I pressed my mouth to his.

His short intake of breath let me know that I'd surprised him. Then, immediately, he groaned quietly, a deep, guttural noise that I felt all the way to my toes. His left hand moved to the back of my head, pulling me closer.

It was perfect, yet restrictive, with the barrier of the console between us. I wanted him closer, wanted to deepen our kiss but I was afraid I'd been too forward by making the first move; Eoghanan was an old-fashioned man, after all. "Wait. I..." My words were shaky. I breathed deeply, trying to catch my breath. "I did that too soon. I'm sorry."

He laughed a bit, but allowed me to pull away. "It was not too soon for me, lass."

I searched his eyes. "But – do you mean –?"

His lips met mine again, silencing my question while, at the same time, answering it. I forgot about the console, about the possibility of cars passing by. He tasted of the wine we'd had at dinner, and smelled of the soap from his earlier shower—clean and all man. His fingers slipped into my hair, and mine slipped into his. I might've stayed there forever, just kissing him, if he hadn't pulled back slightly.

Pressing his forehead to mine, he murmured, "It feels smoother than I even imagined . . . yer hair. And yer lips, so much softer and warmer. I've been wanting this to happen all day, lass, but needed to be certain that ye wanted it, too."

"I wanted it," I whispered, then laughed. "Obviously, right? Seeing as how I gave you no choice."

"I do believe I like it when a woman takes matters into her own hands when a man is too cowardly or too dense to do so. At least, when that woman is you and the man is me." He kissed me again.

"Let me get us back to the inn," I said, unable to stop smiling. "We're going to fog up the car windows if we don't stop, and it isn't even cold out." I sat back, tilting my head to one side as our eyes met. "If you're okay with it, though, I wouldn't mind continuing this later."

He brushed a strand of hair behind my ear and grinned. "Ye wouldn't, aye? Well, I willna deny ye, then."

I couldn't finish the remaining mile fast enough, but after seeing lights still on inside the inn, I parked the car quietly, hoping Cooper wouldn't see us pull up. He'd rush outside to greet us if he did.

We exited the car in sync and after we climbed the steps to the porch, I crushed myself against Eoghanan once again and lost myself in his kiss, not hearing the front door open or the footsteps that approached us.

"Mom, look who's here."

I stilled instantly, mortified that my young son had caught me making out like some hormone-crazed teenager. I didn't even care who was with Cooper; in that moment, I thought nothing could embarrass me more than I already was. I was wrong.

"Tough day at work, Grace?" Jeffrey stood next to Cooper, smiling with shocked eyes.

My ears began to ring, but then Cooper's voice, all high and pitchy with excitement, pierced through the sound. "It's Dad!" he exclaimed.

"Jeffrey!" The pitch of my voice was perilously close to matching Cooper's. Guilt swarmed over me, although there was no reason for it; I'd been doing nothing wrong. Only Eoghanan's horrified expression made me feel like I had.

"This is Cooper's da?" Eoghanan took a huge step away from me, putting a wide gap between us. His gaze darted from Jeffrey to Cooper to me, his brows turning in deeper with each flick of his eyes. "I think I'll retire, Grace," he said, his voice hard. Then he walked away.

I wanted to go after him, but there were other people I had to deal with first. I waited until the inn door closed behind Eoghanan then I stepped forward to hug Cooper and then Jeffrey.

"What are you doing here?" I asked.

"I decided it wasn't worth it to stay and listen to your father. I turned over my clients to other lawyers and decided to join the two of you." Jeffrey winked down at Cooper who was ecstatic at how Mom's business trip had turned into a family vacation for him.

"Oh." I knew Jeffrey could see the disappointment on my face, and I rushed to clarify. "It's not that I'm unhappy to see you. You'll be a big help if you'll keep Cooper occupied while I work. It's just..." I jerked my head back toward the car to indicate the scene that he and Cooper had interrupted. "I just wish you'd waited a minute to make your appearance."

Jeffrey pulled the corner of his lip down in apology. "Yeah, sorry about that. The way Cooper talked about it, I just didn't put it together that it was *that sort* of dinner. Guess you'd better go after him to do some explaining, huh?"

Before I could answer, he bent to pick up Cooper. "You ready to go to bed?" Cooper yawned and lay his head on his dad's shoulder. His excitement had worn him out. Jeffrey turned his attention back to me. "Go, Grace. We can talk more in the morning. The old lady—Morna, right? Anyhow, she put me in my own room. I'll take Cooper with me."

"Ok, thank you." I kissed Jeffrey on the cheek and Cooper on the top of his head, holding open the door for them to pass through.

"Hey, Grace." Jeffrey paused at the base of the stairs, looking at me over his shoulder. "Good on you. It's good to see you smile —get out a bit. It's time."

---

*E*oghanan didn't answer my first knock, so I yelled at him as I rapped my knuckles against the door a second time.

"Look," I called to him. "I know all that took place on the porch didn't make me look so good. Will you open the door so I can explain?"

The handle turned slowly to reveal a stone-faced Eoghanan. He stood blocking the doorway. Clearly, I wouldn't be permitted inside.

"I am angry with ye, Grace. I doona think there is need for explanation. 'Twas verra apparent."

"No, believe me, there's a great need for explanation. It's a complicated situation."

He made a noise that lay somewhere between a groan and a laugh. A noise that gave away the extent of his hurt and anger. "I doona doubt that lass, but I doona wish to hear it. Goodnight."

He shut the door.

The breeze that followed froze my face.

CHAPTER 14

"Good morning." I entered Jeffrey and Cooper's room bearing coffee and orange juice. Although I didn't much feel like it, I couldn't help but smile at the sight of Cooper and his dad coloring together.

Jeffrey stood as I entered, reaching desperately for his coffee. "You're amazing. Thank you. Last night didn't go so well, huh?"

"Why do you say that?" Setting Cooper's orange juice down on the floor next to him, I started in on my own cup of coffee.

"Give me some credit, Grace. I know you." He pointed to my forehead. "That large vein that runs across the top of your head bulges when you're stressed or upset. It's bulging this morning."

"Great." I rubbed at the vein and then stopped, knowing it would only aggravate it more. "You're right, though. He wasn't in the mood to let me explain. I don't know if he'll ever be." Waving a hand dismissively, I took a large gulp of coffee. "Just as well, I guess. It would be a bad idea to get involved. Ya know, since he lives in Scotland and we live in New York."

"What a load of crap, Grace."

Jeffrey was absolutely right, but if I admitted that, I knew I'd get all sad and mopey. I had too much work to do for that.

"No, it's not a load of crap. It's practical. This is a work trip, and that's what I plan on doing today. Coop and I are going to be gone taking photos this afternoon. Want to join us?"

"No. I think I'll hang around here." There was an expression on his face that made me nervous. An expression that said, *I have definite plans, but I'd just rather you didn't know about them.*

"Are you sure? What is there for you to do around here? You're not planning on saying anything to Eoghanan are you? Because there's no point. Please don't."

"Yeah, I'm sure. I plan on sleeping most of the day, not meddling in your dating life."

Dating life. He said it like I usually had one. I didn't think that one date could be considered equivalent to my having a dating life—dating incident, perhaps. "Sleep is the worst thing you can do for your jet lag," I told him. "You'll never adjust to the time change that way."

He rolled his eyes. "I'm adjusted. I'm just exhausted and want to spend a lazy day doing nothing but sleeping and eating."

"Okay, fine. Just don't say anything to him, okay?"

"Sure thing, Grace. Sure thing."

---

*E*oghanan slept fitfully. Visions of Grace's face as her husband walked up on them kissing floated up behind his eyelids each time he tried to shut his eyes. He'd thought over the events of the previous evening repeatedly, each time all of it making less sense than the last.

He'd seen it on her face—the guilt, the regret she felt at kissing him. She'd not been pleased to be seen with him. It had been his mistake to assume Cooper's father was dead. He didn't understand enough of modern-day customs to have another explanation for why the lass and her son would have traveled such a great distance alone.

How ironic that he would be accused of having an affair once when he was innocent, only to be guilty in a different one without his knowledge. It was unfair of Grace to treat him thus, to pull him into such a situation. Surely, he'd not behaved in such a way to make her think he was the kind of man who would kiss another man's wife.

One aspect of the evening confused him more than any other. Why hadn't Grace's husband knocked him on his arse for placing such intimate hands on his wife? Eoghanan certainly would have if the situation had been reversed. Instead, the man had smiled at them both, with no show of anger in his eyes.

As if summoned by mere thought, Eoghanan opened his door to the rough knocking of the very man he'd been thinking about.

The man held the same unsettling smile. Surely it wasn't a common thing in this time for men to share their women so leisurely. The man extended his hand toward Eoghanan. Ignoring the painful pull of his shoulder, Eoghanan met the man's hand with his own.

"Uh, hello. I didn't get to properly introduce myself last night. Name's Jeffrey. Do you mind if I talk to you for a minute?"

"I'm Eoghanan. Aye, come in." Eoghanan stepped aside to allow Jeffrey entry, wondering if now would be when he might swing a fist in his direction. Perhaps he'd only refrained from doing so last night so that young Cooper wouldn't see the altercation.

Once inside the room, Jeffrey faced him. "I need to talk to you about Grace."

Of course, why else would this stranger need to speak with him? "Aye, I believe I owe ye an apology. I willna lay the blame on Grace, but I dinna know that ye were married. I wouldna have...I wouldna have kissed her if I had."

"What? Grace and I are not married. You owe me no apology, not at all. As long as you don't hurt her, you go ahead and kiss Grace all you want to. I imagine it would do her some good."

Jeffrey clasped him on his injured shoulder, and Eoghanan had to clamp down on his teeth to keep from groaning with pain. His head hurt. He'd not felt such an overwhelming lack of understanding in a very long time.

"So, ye are not Grace's husband, but ye are Cooper's father? Forgive me, I doona think I understand the situation."

Jeffrey shrugged and started to make his way back to the doorway. "Yes, I'm Cooper's father, but not Grace's husband. It's a weird situation. Look, I already told Grace I wouldn't say anything to you, so I'm not going to say anything else. I just wanted you to know that whatever conclusion you jumped to last night is undoubtedly wrong. Talk to her."

Eoghanan nodded, unsure of what else to say.

Nodding in return, Jeffrey retreated two steps toward the door before pausing to face him again. "Oh, and one other thing. Grace may not be my wife, but she's my family. I have a strong feeling that you made her cry last night. I didn't see her do it, but this morning her head was all veiny and her eyes all red. That is not okay. You make her cry ever again, and I'll knock you flat on your ass. I don't care if you're eight inches taller than me. Got it?"

Eoghanan repressed a grin. Stranger or not, anyone who would rise to Grace's defense in such a manner had his respect and admiration. "Aye."

"Good. Well then, have a good day. See ya around."

Jeffrey turned and left, leaving Eoghanan smiling in the doorway. He'd gather more explanation from Grace later. He'd already heard the most important part—the lass wasn't married, and so his own hope could remain.

CHAPTER 15

After I'd spoken with Jeffrey, I spent the rest of the day working. I drove down the road to Conall Castle, allowing Cooper to show me the best places to take pictures after he told me he'd looked around especially for them during his trip there with Jerry and Morna. While not the first places I would have chosen to photograph, it thrilled me that my son was so thoughtful. I gladly followed him around, letting him lead me for the day.

By the time we returned to the inn, Coop was more than ready to spend some time with his dad, which gave me the evening to work on the article. I worked steadily, determined to keep my mind off of Eoghanan and my frustration that he had not allowed me to explain myself. As much as I wanted to hash things out, I'd spent too much of my childhood around a man who wouldn't listen to what I had to say whenever I needed him to hear me the most. Though I didn't believe this was a common character trait of Eoghanan's, his refusal to listen made me feel like the repressed child, teenager, and then young mom that I'd once been. I was finished trying to reason with someone who didn't want to hear me.

I heard a rapid pounding at my door. Jeffrey always knocked in the same way—three taps, brief silence, followed by three more taps. Cooper never knocked and neither did Morna or Jerry, so as soon as I heard the noise at my door, I knew who to expect. Eoghanan. Part of me had known that Jeffrey wouldn't keep his promise. Subconsciously, I think that's why I asked it of him. I had secretly hoped he'd speak to Eoghanan and explain what I hadn't been allowed to.

Taking a breath, I stood, closed my laptop, and readied myself to give Eoghanan a full explanation, even if Jeffrey already had. Not that I believed it would make any real difference, no matter how much I wanted it to. Still, I couldn't bear the thought of Eoghanan believing me a liar or a cheat. My little family—Jeffrey, Cooper, and me—was unusual and difficult for anyone outside it to really understand. It was part of the reason I'd avoided the dating scene since Cooper's birth. I didn't want to have to explain how it worked, to promise over and over that nothing was going on between Jeffrey and me, that nothing ever had.

"Grace, I need to speak to ye if ye will allow it, lass."

"Of course I will." Swinging open the door, I stepped aside so he would enter. I closed the door behind him, and to my surprise, turned right into his arms.

He hugged me tightly, apologizing with his chin against the top of my head. "I am not a good man, Grace. I dinna know what to think when wee Cooper and Jeffrey walked up on us, but I should have allowed ye to explain. 'Tis only that I'd not felt as happy in ages as I did when I held ye in my arms. When I learned that Jeffrey is Cooper's father— believing that ye'd lied to me—it hurt me more deeply than I'd like to admit. I dinna behave as I should have."

I rubbed his back gently with my hand, speaking against his chest. "I'm sorry, too. It just seemed a bit early to explain everything, and I never thought Jeffrey would show up here. He talked to you, I guess?"

He nodded, and his chin felt much more boney against my head than it truly was.

"What did he tell you?"

I couldn't see Jeffrey getting into too deep of an explanation. While he spoke to me about everything, he wasn't that way with most people. I imagined he would have told Eoghanan only what was necessary to convince him to let me explain.

Eoghanan released me and paced around the room a bit, confirming what I'd already guessed. Jeffrey had told him little. Eoghanan still appeared quite confused by the entire situation.

"Not verra much. He said that 'twas yer story to tell, and he's right. I should have allowed ye to do so. All Jeffrey told me was that ye are not married to him, which is what I thought when Cooper called him Da."

"Well..." I moved to sit on the end of my bed, patting the mattress so that he would join me. Before last night, I would have worried about Cooper walking in and seeing a man in his mother's room. But now that his father was here, Coop had gleefully moved into his dad's bedroom to spend his nights there. "I almost was. Just last week, actually."

"Ah." I watched as Eoghanan's body tensed slightly, but he still moved to sit next to me. "So ye are not married to him, but ye are his?"

Placing Jeffrey inside any sort of context where I belonged to him made me squirm internally. I shook my head, reaching for both of Eoghanan's hands. "No. If you don't hear anything else I say, hear that. Jeffrey and I are not an item and we *never* have been."

His thick brows pulled in tight. He was trying to understand what I meant, but was, of course, having trouble. "But ye have a child together."

"Yes, but we didn't...Jeffrey isn't Cooper's real father." I looked down at our hands, mine squeezing his tightly, his thumb moving back and forth as it had when we were together last night.

He exhaled loudly, as if he'd been holding his breath for a long time. We sat there, each of us avoiding the other's gaze, our heart rates slowly escalating, the tension between us building once again.

Eventually, he pulled one of his hands away, moving it to my chin as he lifted my face to make me look at him. "I still doona think I understand all there is to know, but ye are saying that ye and Jeffrey are not married and willna ever be. That ye are not spoken for by anyone else, aye?"

I couldn't help but smile. Spoken for? It seemed archaic language. Why didn't he just say, 'Are you dating anyone else?' Regardless, Eoghanan said many things in such a way, and he made it sound charming every time. "Yes, that is what I'm saying." I held eye contact, determined not to break it so that he would understand that point. "I am entirely single."

"I am pleased to hear it, lass."

"Do you want to hear the rest?" I pulled away a bit so I could kick off my shoes and pull my legs beneath me to settle into a more comfortable position.

"Aye. Verra much so."

"Okay."

And so I began. I told him about my father's job, the old money from which he came, not to mention the mounds of money he had made on his own – all of it combining to create our family's New York estate. How I'd grown up surrounded by unimaginable, disgusting wealth, and that Jeffrey, along with his father, had been the primary grounding force throughout my entire life.

"I met Jeffrey when I was four. My father hired both his parents; his mother to work as a maid in our household, and his father to manage our grounds. The family moved into one of the small cottages on our estate. Since Jeffrey and I were the same age, we just took to each other." I paused, checking out Eoghanan's expression to make certain he hadn't grown bored. It wasn't the shortest of stories, but he couldn't have appeared more attentive.

He patted my hand gently. "Go on, lass. I wish to hear everything."

Nodding, I said, "I grew to love Jeffrey and his parents as if they were my own family, spending more time in their cottage than our mansion because I felt wanted there. I was close to my sisters, and to a lesser degree, my mom, but we were a house divided. All of us girls versus my dad. It made for a cold, stressed, disingenuous environment.

"Jeffrey's family did everything under a canopy of the love they felt for one another, and it was contagious. Jeffrey's mother died when we were eight, and it was the most devastating event of my childhood. I remember thinking that I was more heartbroken at her death than I would have been at my own father's because I knew that Maggie loved me. To this day, I don't know that about my father."

I swallowed the lump that rose in my throat.

"Anyway, Jeffrey and I leaned on each other a lot during that time. He became my brother, my best friend, and we've just always stayed like that. In college, I started dating an exchange student from Australia. He was a real loser, and deep down I knew that. But after years of trying to be perfect, I wanted something wild, something fun. The Aussie definitely was that. Jeffrey couldn't stand him, but the guy did end up giving me the one thing I care most about in the entire world—Cooper."

I sighed, the memory of my relationship with Cooper's biological father never a pleasant one.

"When I told him I was pregnant, he bounced. As in, he actually left and flew back home to Australia. I never heard from him after that. Jeffrey stepped in even before I told my family. And now..." I was ready to finish my explanation. Talking about myself wasn't my favorite thing to do by any stretch of the imagination. "Jeffrey is Cooper's dad in every way that matters.

But, Jeffrey and I . . . he's my best friend, not my lover. Never has been."

I breathed deeply. It was a relief to tell him. As much as I had tried to busy myself with work, I'd remained anxious all day, wanting to talk to him and explain.

"Thank ye for telling me, lass. May I ask ye one more question?"

I nodded, feeling sleepy now that my previous anxiety melted away.

"Then why did ye and Jeffrey almost marry?"

"Oh. Gosh." I rubbed my eyelids with my thumb and middle finger. My almost-marriage to Jeffrey seemed so much like a bad dream that it still didn't seem real to me. "My father had taken a liking to Jeffrey once he saw what a great father he was to Cooper and talked him into going to law school. He even paid for it. Once Jeffrey graduated, he made him a partner at his law firm. And then he decided that just wasn't good enough, so he blackmailed us. He said it wasn't right for a partner at his firm to have a child and not be married. We went along with it, right up until the wedding day. But we couldn't do it. The real kicker is that Jeffrey doesn't even want to be a lawyer. He did that for me, too, because my father expected it of him."

"I doona think I am fond of yer father, lass."

I snorted. "Join the club."

Eoghanan stood, moving toward the door. It wasn't what I expected, for him to hear my explanation and leave so soon, but I was quickly learning that he was anything but predictable. "Can ye stand up for me, lass?"

I did, stepping toward him. "Why?"

"We were interrupted last evening, aye?"

Hesitantly, I moved closer, my chest all fluttery inside. "Yes."

"Do ye think we might be interrupted again?"

I closed my eyes for a long second, allowing the trickle of

anticipation to travel along my spine. "No. Cooper's with his dad."

He reached me in one long step and drew me to him. It felt as if my entire body sighed as he kissed me. A slow, sweet kiss that washed away every other thought outside of his touch.

We kissed until both of us were weak from it, breathless. Then, surprising me with his abruptness, Eoghanan pulled away and moved quickly to open the door.

"I'll leave ye, lass. 'Tis not the time for more, and if I stay . . ."

He didn't need to finish the statement; I understood. I nodded, agreeing on an intellectual basis, but already missing his touch. "Right. You're right, though I wish that you weren't."

"Ach, I wish the same." He turned away from me and began his trek down the hall. "Sleep well, lass," he said over his shoulder. "For I know that I willna do so."

CHAPTER 16

I don't know if it was relief at having things sorted out with Eoghanan or my subconscious taking advantage of the fact that having Jeffrey here released me from having to be on constant Cooper-watch, but I slept later than usual and woke feeling utterly relaxed.

After a quick shower and a messy hair fix, I walked downstairs to find everyone visiting happily in the living room. Cooper had roped Jerry into getting down onto the floor with him, and I silently worried about the old man's knees. He didn't seem the least bit bothered by them, though, as he dramatically role-played with Coop's dinosaurs.

"Mom! I thought you were gonna sleep all day, lazy head," shrieked Cooper. Pausing their game, he ran to greet me. I scooped him up in my arms, kissing him firmly on the top of his head.

"All day? I might have slept a little later, but it's only eight in the morning. What time did you get up?"

"Oh, I don't know, the usual time."

"I know." Jeffrey turned to answer me, his eyes still sleepy, rounded out by dark circles. Clearly, Cooper hadn't given his father the same courtesy he usually gave me by occupying himself for a while. "It was four. Four a.m., and he's jacked up like he had six cups of coffee."

I played with Coop's messy curls as I set him back down on his feet. "Well, if four a.m. really is the usual time, I never did set my alarm that early. I truly don't know how you do it, Coop."

He shrugged, looking up at me with a grin. "I don't know either, Mom. I really don't. I guess I'm just too excited for all the things I gotta do each day to sleep."

I laughed at his beautiful attitude and hoped he'd keep it always. "I guess so." I turned my attention to everyone else in the room, catching Eoghanan's eye for the first time this morning.

He smiled at me, but not widely enough so as to draw attention from everyone else. His eyes, although nearly as tired as Jeffrey's, looked excited and happy. I hadn't felt that way in such a long time—that feeling of being in a room with many people, but being so intensely aware of just one person that it's as if there's a secret between the two of you that no one else knows. The promise of another encounter if you can just find the time to sneak away together. I hoped that the opportunity would come for us very soon.

Eventually, I pulled my eyes away and willed myself to speak, addressing the room as a whole. "What's on everybody's agenda? How about we all drive to McMillan Castle and explore around there for the day?"

"McMillan Castle? Why there, lass?" Eoghanan seemed shocked by my suggestion, though I couldn't imagine why.

"For the article. It looks lovely on the Internet, and I'd like to check it out. Do you know it?"

"Aye." Eoghanan shared a knowing glance with Morna, puzzling me further. "I know it verra well, lass. 'Tis a good way from here."

"Farther than Edinburgh?" I couldn't begin to rationalize his reaction. As much time as he'd spent in the inn, I'd expected him to jump at any excuse to get out for a while. Instead, he seemed genuinely hesitant. Even more than that, he seemed afraid to go there.

"No, 'tis closer than Edinburgh."

"Is it haunted or something?" I laughed, but his face showed he didn't think my question very funny.

"Not for ye, though it might be for myself." He said it softly, almost underneath his breath.

I wasn't given the chance to ask him what he meant by that statement, for as soon as he spoke, Morna leapt up from the couch, saying, "I think it's a lovely idea, Grace. We should leave soon, for it isna a short ride. Cooper," she tapped him gently on the shoulder, "would ye mind helping me make some sandwiches to pack? Jerry, why doona ye and Jeffrey ready the cars? Grace, ye go pack yer camera."

Everyone dispersed quickly, and I was left with little choice but to do the same. I hesitated, lingering in the doorway until it was only Eoghanan and me in the living room. "Are you okay?"

He nodded, standing and moving forward to grab my hand, squeezing it gently. "Aye. McMillan Castle is lovely. 'Tis only..." He hesitated far too long, finally releasing my hand as he turned away, ending the conversation. "Never mind, lass. Go and get yer things. 'Tis nothing to worry yerself over."

Knowing when to leave well enough alone, I stepped away, wondering all the way to my room just what had been said during the other conversation in the living room.

The conversation that had been entirely silent.

---

*E*oghanan wanted to tell her desperately just why he didn't wish to go to McMillan Castle. That he didn't wish to see his home, the castle he'd grown up in, crawling with visitors, no longer a home or safe haven among the Highlands. All of it a painful reminder that, while he knew his family lived in the past, in today's time they'd all been dead for hundreds of years.

A hand gripped his shoulder, pulling him from his thoughts. Morna stood next to him, her knowing eyes telling him she suspected and understood his concerns.

"Ye needn't worry. I too once had trouble visiting my old home. But now, seeing all that it is today gives me comfort that harm dinna befall all those I love over the centuries. McMillan Castle is still in fine condition today; ye will be surprised to find that many things still look much the same. And..." She patted his right hand, where he gripped the spelled rock that had sent him here. "If ye are worried that I'll spell ye back, I have no intention of doing so today. Not when ye are just getting to know the lass. Besides, ye still need to heal, and ye have some time before Mitsy's babe is born."

"Thank ye." Eoghanan turned the rock over in his hand, realizing that perhaps leaving had been his greatest fear. He couldn't go home just yet, not before he'd told Grace the truth.

Smiling, Morna stepped toward the hallway. "Still, I think it best ye leave the wee rock here. Ye wouldna want someone throwing it into the pond by happenchance."

"No, I wouldna."

The old woman turned to leave as he placed the rock down, and he called out to stop her. "Morna, will she believe me?"

"Grace? Ye care verra much about the lass, aye?"

Eoghanan nodded. "Aye, far too much. And too soon, as well."

"There is no such thing as too soon if 'tis a match that is destined. While Grace doesna know it yet, ye do, I can tell. 'Tis destined, lad, so though she might need some help, when ye decide to tell her, she'll believe ye in time.

*C*ooper couldn't see Morna and Eoghanan, but he listened attentively, his back flat against the side of the kitchen wall. *Please don't let Mom catch me. Please don't let Mom catch me.* He repeated the words over and over again in his mind, not wishing to be caught eavesdropping once again.

Waiting until E-o's heavy footsteps walked up the stairs and Morna's voice hollered after Jerry as she exited the front door, he silently made his way into the living room.

He knew Mom liked E-o. He'd never seen her get dressed up so nice just for dinner. Cooper liked E-o, too. He even thought that maybe Dad liked him.

If Mom needed help believing in the magic, then he'd be the perfect helper.

He'd noticed the black, shiny rock E-o had held this morning. Now the rock lay on the small table in the center of the room. Sticking his head out in the hallway and looking both directions for good measure, he scurried quietly over to the table.

Picking up the rock, he slipped it securely away in the pocket of his jeans.

CHAPTER 17

M cMillan Castle—Present Day

Eoghanan imagined ghosts felt much the same way when they traveled the halls of their homes, silently watching over loved ones. As he roamed through the empty dining hall now lit with the same electrical hanging lamps that hung from the ceilings of Morna's home, a strange realization hit him; although he couldn't see them, he imagined that his family was eating right at this moment in this very room—only hundreds of years in the past. They wouldn't know that he stood among them, but would be oblivious of his unseen presence so many years in the future.

Shaking his head to push the nostalgia away, Eoghanan wandered up the stairs to his old bedchamber, continuing his search for Cooper as he'd promised the boy he would. Trying to remember what the lad had told him to call in warning, he spoke out to the empty room. "Ready or not, here I come."

The room truly did look much the same, thanks to many rounds of restorations. Red ropes lined the furnishings to keep visitors from coming too near. He and Cooper ignored the ropes entirely during their game of hide-and-seek. Thanks to Morna, they were the only visitors at the castle this day, and it had become their playground.

Eoghanan stepped over the rope to open a chest near the foot of the bed. It wasn't his, but one much like it. Cooper sat crouched down inside of it.

"Found ye."

"Oh, man! I thought this was such a good hiding place. How do you keep finding me?"

Eoghanan looked around to ensure that Grace hadn't wandered in on them. "Have ye kept our secret, Cooper?"

"About the magic and you being like really, really old and stuff? Yeah, of course I have."

Eoghanan laughed loudly, the sound of it echoing off the walls. "I am not verra old, Cooper. Why do ye think that?"

The young boy held his hands palms up, shrugging a bit as he spoke. "Well, if you can travel in time and you were born close to the dinosaurs, then you're really old."

"Not verra close to the dinosaurs, but 'tis not my point. If ye have kept the secret this long, perhaps I can tell ye another, aye?"

"Yeah, I can keep it."

"This castle is where I was born. In my own time, 'tis where I live. This is my own bedchamber."

Cooper's eyes widened. "Awwwesome. So, when are you gonna tell Mom?"

It was the very question he'd asked himself all day. This castle —his home—seemed the best place to do so since it was the place he loved most in the world. "I doona know," he admitted to Cooper.

"Don't you like her?"

Eoghanan smiled, taking Cooper by the hand and walking toward the staircase where they sat down next to one another.

"Aye, I like her verra much. 'Tis why I doona know if I should tell her, even though I want to."

Cooper regarded him skeptically. "That doesn't make any sense, E-o."

"Aye, ye may be right. Ye see, we are still verra new to each other, yer mother and I, but I care about her verra much. That doesna mean that she feels the same way about me. If I did tell her about the magic, 'twould be so that she might consider returning home with me—along with ye and yer father, if ye wish it. She's only known me a week."

"A week is a real long time."

Cooper sat with his elbows on his knees, his palms cupping his small face. He was an intelligent child; fun, curious, kind. In that moment, Eoghanan knew that he loved him. The boy's presence awakened a desire within him to be a father—a desire he'd not known was hiding within him. If he could love the boy after only a week, why couldn't he love the boy's mother, as well?

"Do ye really think a week is a long time?"

Eoghanan waited patiently, appreciating how Cooper always took time before answering a question. He thought about things deeply. At such a young age, the boy had already mastered a talent possessed by far too few adults.

Finally, Cooper asked, "Well, are we talkin' about love here?"

Eoghanan smiled, nodding silently.

"Then, yeah . . . A week is *real* long. Let me think... When Bebop tells me something I don't understand, he tells me a story to help me get it. You wanna hear a story, E-o?"

"Aye, tell me yer story."

"I don't know if you know this, but next to Mom, Dad, and Bebop, I love dinosaurs more than anything else in the world. He spread his arms wide. "I love them soooo much, and it didn't take me a week to figure that out. I knew the first time I saw a dinosaur in a book my Bebop got for me that I loved them. Not everybody loves dinosaurs. Grandfather doesn't, but that's okay.

'Cause I was *meant* to love dinosaurs. What I mean is, if you and my mom are also meant to love each other, then a week is a long time to know it."

Eoghanan shook his head in disbelief. "How old are ye again, Cooper?"

Cooper tapped the side of his head. "I know, I'm kinda weird. I think my brain is older than my body."

Eoghanan laughed. "I doona doubt it. Ye are a verra special lad. I have never met a child like ye before."

"Does that mean you're gonna tell her?"

Eoghanan stood, jerking his head toward the castle's main entrance. "Aye, I think I shall. Let's go and join the others. Do ye mind staying with yer father a while, so that I may talk to yer mother alone?"

"Yeah, sure. Maybe Dad will play hide-and-seek."

"Aye, perhaps he will. I think it may take some time to explain the magic to yer mother. Even then, I doona know if she will believe me."

Cooper took off down the stairs, hollering over his shoulder, "Don't worry about that, E-o. I'll help you with that part. If she doesn't believe you, I think I know something that will work."

Eoghanan couldn't explain it, but as Cooper ran out the front door of the castle, a sense of unease settled over him.

CHAPTER 18

Much to all of our delight, when we arrived at McMillan Castle around noon, there was not a single tourist to be found on the grounds. It was literally as if the place had been vacated just for us. The only person on the property, as far as I could tell, was a lackadaisical ticket operator who seemed much too interested in her magazine to worry about what areas we did and did not enter. We had free run of the place, which made for excellent picture taking. While Jerry, Morna, and Jeffrey visited with each other by the pond out front, Eoghanan occupied Coop with a castle-sized game of hide and seek. McMillan Castle was a magnificent edifice, and I was glad to get some work done, but I was even more pleased when Cooper came running outside again and headed straight for his dad.

Eoghanan made his way out more slowly, lingering near the entryway of the castle. Something in my gut started to hum each time I saw him. I barely knew him, but I kept trying to think of reasons to call Mr. Perdie to ask if I could extend the length of my trip. I still had a week left here, but I was beginning to believe that no amount of time would ever feel like enough. It was completely irrational thinking; on the drive here, I realized I didn't even know Eoghanan's last name. I knew nothing about his family or even what he did for a living. The one thing I did know for certain was that, no matter when I left here, I would think about him every day for the rest of my life.

Still, that wasn't enough. There was something mysterious about the man that I couldn't figure out. Until I did, I wouldn't allow myself to trust my feelings for him. I knew myself well enough to admit that, despite my lack of romance in recent years, I always had a tendency to fall for bad guys—the kind who purposely leave important details about themselves out of the conversation. The kind who are more attractive because of their mysteriousness rather than their substance.

I could tell by Eoghanan's eyes—Cooper and Bebop were right about people's eyes—that he couldn't be lumped into the same "bad guy" group as so many others. Regardless, he still remained too much of an enigma for me to open up to him completely.

His injury, although partially explained, still made very little sense to me. Who in the heck got into sword fights nowadays? And what could he possibly have done to provoke one? Not to mention his odd speech and his obvious fascination with the car. If I didn't know better, I'd think he'd never ridden in a vehicle before.

And although I'd put off his reaction to Jeffrey's arrival as being more out of surprise at the situation than true anger, it seemed weird to me that he would assume that just because Jeffrey was Cooper's father that he and I were married. With divorce being so common, wouldn't the most obvious conclusion be that Jeffrey and I were no longer married, rather than that I was a cheating spouse?

Lastly, Cooper's small mention of a secret between him and Eoghanan nagged at the back of my mind relentlessly. I knew it had to be innocent enough, but I couldn't help but wonder if the so-called secret was somehow related to Cooper's belief that Eoghanan was the man he saw at the park and the airport. I knew my son, and he was not one to let things go. If Cooper believed something, he wouldn't allow it to be dismissed without proper explanation, and he'd dropped the issue suddenly, right after his fishing trip with Jerry and Eoghanan.

I liked Eoghanan...a lot. I loved talking to him. I loved how much Cooper adored him. And despite how it made me feel like a lovestruck teenager, I couldn't be near him without daydreaming about him holding me in his arms and kissing me until my toes curled. Still, I needed to know a lot more, and very soon, or I would have no reason to stay past the end of the week—even if he wanted me to. As of yet, he'd said nothing of the sort, so maybe I was worrying over nothing.

I smiled as I approached him, hoping he couldn't see all the thoughts running wild behind my eyes. "Hey, you. Everything all right?"

His face was serious and a bit apprehensive as he took my hand and began to pull me away from the others, toward the side of the castle. "Aye, come with me."

Allowing myself one quick glance backward to make sure Cooper was being supervised, I faced him again, allowing him to lead the way. It struck me as odd that he moved with such direction. Without a doubt, he'd been here before. "Where are we going?"

"There is a tree near the back with a large branch that nearly touches the ground. I go there often to think."

"Often?" How could that be? He'd told me more than once that he lived quite far from the inn. While the castle was a several-hour drive, he'd spoken about his home as if it were much further away than this. Had he lied and that was why he'd been so hesitant to come here? "Are you from near here?"

He turned suddenly toward me, blocking the path. "Aye, in a

way I am from both verra near here and verra far away." He tilted his head to one side, his eyes narrowing. "Do ye believe in magic, lass?"

What a weird question. I stuttered a little, unsure of what he meant by 'magic.' "Do you mean, like, a higher power? If so, yes, I do. But if you're referring to hocus pocus stuff, I've not ever seen evidence of it, so I would have to say I don't know. I do think things happen all the time that have no logical explanation, and perhaps those things are the result of a kind of magic. Why?"

Perhaps the magic he spoke of lay within him, for I couldn't help but feel as if he'd read my mind. While the direction of the conversation made me uneasy, I had a feeling I would finally be granted some answers.

He said nothing until we reached the tree. After he sat down, he pulled me in next to him. "I'd like to tell ye something...my surname is McMillan."

"Oh." It seemed an odd build up for such a small piece of information, then I remembered where we were. My brows lifted. "Oh. Ooohhh..." Each time I said the word a little louder, as if some sort of grand realization came over me...it didn't. "So, you didn't grow up quite as far from the inn as I thought, although I guess that all depends on your perspective. Does your family own this? Your ancestors were, what? Scottish lairds or something?"

"Aye, they were, but not only my ancestors. My brother is laird of this castle now."

"Your brother." It wasn't so much a question as a statement while I thought about what he could mean. This was the first I'd heard of him having a brother. While I supposed the guy could still be a laird by title, if his family did still own the castle, I didn't think it would be anything more than just that...a title. "Okay, so does your family live near here? Sort of oversee things?"

Eoghanan began to cross his arms, but stopped as his shoulder pulled. "We doona live near it. We live in the castle, lass."

I quickly grew frustrated. I'd taken the same self-guided tour of the place he had, and it was obvious that no one actually still lived in the castle. Furthermore, if they did, why hadn't he said anything while we were walking through it? Why hadn't he told us stories or talked about the castle's history, his ancestors, anything?

I shook my head and frowned. "Eoghanan, I walked through that castle just a while ago, and there's no one living there now."

Eoghanan stood and started pacing back and forth in front of me. He looked as frustrated as I felt. "Do ye remember what Cooper said about me when ye first arrived here?"

I pulled my jacket around me more snugly. There was little wind, but my body temperature seemed to drop suddenly. "Which part? When he mistook you for someone else? He thought he saw you at the airport, but obviously that wasn't you."

"Aye, lass. It was."

---

*C*ooper ran up to his dad, who stood by the pond waving at Morna and Jerry as they pulled away from the castle. "Where are they going?"

"They're just heading back a little early so Morna can get started on some dinner. We'll ride back with Eoghanan and your mom after they finish up whatever they're doing."

Cooper reached down into his pocket, turning the stone over and over, thinking about the magic. It was taking Mom and E-o too long. E-o had been right; his Mom was too much of a grown-up to believe. He would have to help her.

He pulled out the stone, trying to remember what he'd heard Morna say. He couldn't remember exactly, but it was something about the rock touching water. If the rock was magical, his mom would be angry with him for sure, but it was the only way to show her. Besides, it might not do anything—just like the colored dinosaur eggs his Dad had gotten him once. They were supposed to hatch if placed in water, but they never did.

If only grown-ups were easier to teach things to, he wouldn't have had to take the rock in the first place. Rearing back, he let the rock fly toward the pond. The moment it hit the water, everything went black.

CHAPTER 19

"I'm sorry, can you say that again?" Obviously, Eoghanan had misspoken. There was absolutely no way he'd been in the airport. Jerry and Morna had both said he'd been at the inn for several months. He didn't strike me as the type of man who would take off for a quick little "vacay" to New York.

"Grace, I know that ye willna believe me. Not until ye witness it for yerself. 'Tis my hope that ye will allow me to tell ye all that I know and then consider allowing me to prove it to ye."

"Witness what? Eoghanan, you're freaking me out. Just say whatever it is you're trying to say, and say it plainly." I blew out a frustrated breath. "Get on with it."

"I was injured by a sword, just as I told ye, but 'twas not in this time. This wound," he paused to point at the scar that started on the side of his temple, "was given to me in the year sixteen hundred and forty-seven in the verra castle behind ye. I am only in this time now so that I can heal with the help of Morna's magic."

"All right." I stood and blurted out a laugh, tossing a hand in dismissal as I started off in the direction of the pond. "I've had enough. Do you think I'm cra—"

The word hung unfinished when I saw Jeffrey running toward us, dripping wet, breathless, and screaming. Screaming for me to follow him. Eoghanan and I hurried after him as he turned back toward the pond.

"What's wrong?" I yelled. "Where's Cooper?"

Continuing to run, he looked over his shoulder and yelled back, "He's gone, Grace—I— "

"What do you mean, he's gone?" My stomach churned, and the panic building in me made me feel the need to throw up.

We reached the pond and stopped running. "I don't know, Grace. He was standing right there. Right there, Grace." Jeffrey pointed at the grass next to me. He was crying now, tears flowing freely, his voice a panicked rasp. "I was right next to him. He just threw a rock. I swear. I didn't turn away from him for a second. He just threw a rock and..." He shook his head, as if he didn't believe his own words. "He just vanished."

"Jeffrey, if Cooper put you up to this and you were stupid enough to go along with it, I swear to you, I will murder you."

"Grace!" He grabbed me roughly, shaking me so hard my teeth rattled. "Do I look like I'm joking?" He didn't, not at all, and my brain simply couldn't process the horror of what he said. "He's gone, Grace. I don't know how or where or why."

"No. No, no, no, no, no, no, no." I could say nothing else as I collapsed against him.

"Hush, lass." Eoghanan stood behind me, pulling me off of Jeffrey. He gripped my shoulders too tightly, but it was enough to make me do as he said. "Jeffrey, show me what the lad did."

He was so calm I wanted to slap him. I felt as if I was living a nightmare; I wanted to scream, *needed* to scream, but I couldn't make a sound. I twisted away from his grip, whirling on him, my voice barely forming words. "What's...what's the matter with you? We don't have time for this. We have to find him."

I started toward the water to search inside the pond for Cooper, but Eoghanan reached out, jerking me back against him with his left hand, wrapping it around my waist so that I couldn't move.

"Jeffrey," he said firmly, "pick up a rock and show me what the lad did."

Eoghanan's tone was deeper than I'd ever heard it, his words a direct order.

I struggled against him, but he held me still as Jeffrey looked at him, confusion and shock muddling his normally flawless face. Slowly, he bent to pick up a rock. Shaking his head, he drew his hand back. "He just...all he did was throw it."

Jeffrey's rock went sailing toward the water. When it hit the surface and disappeared below the water, so did Jeffrey.

I screamed, and something hard hit me on the top of the head, causing my vision to blur. The last thing I saw before I lost consciousness was the sight of headlights barreling toward us.

CHAPTER 20

The Inn Near Conall Castle—Present Day

"What in the blethering hell did ye do to her, Morna?"

My eyes remained closed, and though I tried to open them, they wouldn't budge. The same could be said for every other part of my body. Someone must have sedated me, for I couldn't lift my arms or legs, open my eyes, or speak. I could do nothing but listen to all they said.

"Calm down, Eoghanan. I just put her to sleep for a while. We wouldna have been able to get her in the car otherwise."

"Ye needed to explain to her what happened, not kidnap the lass."

I could feel Eoghanan running his hand through my hair, and I knew that I lay slumped against him.

"Kidnap her?" Morna's voice sounded appalled at the accusation. "Doona ye blame me for this mess. I told ye not to bring the rock, dinna I?"

"Aye, and I did leave it. Cooper must have picked it up behind me. I thought ye had to skip the rock for it take ye back. Surely the lad couldna do that."

Cooper. His name jolted my memory of what had happened, and I knew I was more than only physically sedated. My son was gone. I'd seen Jeffrey vanish before me, yet the panic I should be feeling wouldn't come. I felt eerily at peace, unworried, sleepy. I fought the urge to give in to unconsciousness by listening intently and trying to understand.

"Aye, 'tis usually true the rock must be skipped," Morna replied. "But I made it so that those needing to travel would have the ability to do so. Cooper must be meant to travel back if it allowed him to simply throw it and not skip it, nor float it like ye did."

"What about Jeffrey?" It was Jerry's voice now, speaking up for the first time.

"Ach, ye saw how quickly I turned the car around. I felt it the moment Cooper traveled back and immediately spelled the other rocks so that someone could follow him."

"How did ye know one of us would throw it?" Eoghanan's voice again.

"I dinna know. 'Twas all I could think to do until we got to ye."

"Aye, fine. When ye arrived, why dinna ye send Grace and me back right away?"

All of this talk of 'back' made little sense, but I was unable to ask questions. I felt paralyzed.

"Eoghanan, ye know that ye are in no shape to travel so far back yet. Grace's arrival has delayed yer progress. We have not been working consistently to regain your strength."

"It no longer matters if I am ready or not. Grace willna wait for me to heal to get to her son, and I willna let her go back without me."

"Aye, I know. 'Tis why I dinna send ye back there. If ye must go, and I know that ye must, I will make sure ye are tended to as best as ye can be before making the journey. Now, rest yer eyes a while, lad. We've much to do when we get back to the inn."

As their voices quieted, so did my ability to stay awake. I allowed sleep to take me, hoping as I drifted that when next I woke, I would be able to feel something other than the strange, disturbing calm settling over me now.

***

"All right, lass, time for ye to wake up now."

Morna's voice called to me from beside my bed. My eyelids flickered open slowly.

I lay in my bed at the inn. Jerry sat at its end, Eoghanan on my right side rubbing my hand gently, and Morna on my left side regarding me closely.

I concentrated on trying to open my mouth, pleased to find that I could. After stretching my jaw a moment, I said, "You all need to tell me exactly what is going on. Where is my son?" While I could move my body, I still felt just as calm as before, and I hated it. Intellectually, I knew something was very wrong, yet I was unable to feel any emotion, and that disturbed me greatly.

Morna nodded. "Aye, 'tis exactly what we intend to do. Ye may notice that ye feel a bit calm. 'Tis only something I've done so ye will sit still long enough to hear everything. It will recede slowly, but if ye lose yer cool, Grace, I'll spell ye again."

"Spell me?" My tone came off as sarcastic, although after everything that had taken place today, I was inclined to believe her.

"Aye, lass. Spell ye. I'm a witch, and quite a powerful one." Morna extended a glass of water in my direction. I took it, sitting up in the bed.

Eoghanan sighed loudly. "'Tis what I meant to tell ye, when..." He trailed off.

My thoughts went right back to Cooper and Jeffrey. "Where are they?"

By the way he kept fumbling with my fingers, I could tell that Eoghanan was nervous. I didn't understand why. I wouldn't get upset no matter what he said. I was entirely incapable of it. As soon as I could feel again, I knew I would be spitfire angry at being repressed in such a manner.

"They're still at McMillan Castle," he said. "But with my family, in the seventeenth century."

I narrowed my eyes skeptically. "Of course they are. So Morna is a witch, and you're a time traveler." I turned my eyes on Jerry. "What are you? A goblin?"

The old man frowned at me. "I take offense to that, lass. Do I look like a goblin?"

I didn't answer him, instead looking at Eoghanan for further explanation.

"'Tis like I told ye, Grace. I was only sent here after I almost died. My brother is married to a lass from this time; her name is Mitsy. Morna sent her back, as well. When I was injured, she knew that Morna could save me and sent me forward to her."

"Okay." I couldn't argue with him. No matter how ridiculous it sounded, no matter how unbelievable, I had seen Jeffrey vanish. There was no doubt in my mind about that. "So why were you at the airport? And the park? Before Jeffrey...you said that Cooper was right about seeing you. Have you been stalking us?"

"No." It was Morna who answered, rising quickly to Eoghanan's defense. "Of course he has not been stalking ye. 'Twas me that sent him to ye."

She glanced over at Eoghanan. "Aye, ye heard me, lad; I lied to ye. I do control where ye go on yer travels."

Returning her attention to me, she continued, "The span of time between now and his world was too great with his wound. The spell and the resulting travel rips ye apart a bit."

I swallowed, thinking of Cooper, grateful for the first time that I couldn't feel anything.

Eoghanan must have been able to follow my train of thought, for he interrupted Morna as he thumbed my hand, a comforting gesture. "Do ye really think that is what ye needed to tell her just now? With her worried about wee Cooper?"

Morna nodded, dismissing him. "Aye, she needed to know so I could explain why ye dinna go straight home. Besides, she is not worried about anything at the moment." I hated that she was right. "Back to what I was saying to ye, lass. I have been slowly building his strength in the travel, though it seems there is no more time for that. I know ye are ready to see that yer boy is well. In just a moment, I will remove the spell from ye, and we will prepare Eoghanan right away."

"Prepare him?" After Morna's description, I could just imagine Eoghanan being ripped apart, only to have his fragile skin not come back together properly. "If he's not ready, I can go by myself. I just want to make sure Cooper is okay." I looked at Eoghanan. "I don't want you getting hurt. I can go alone."

He kissed my hand gently and reached up to brush a lock of hair out of my eyes. "Ye are mad if ye think I would let ye do that, lass. I'm going."

Morna stood abruptly, nodding as she waved to Jerry so he'd follow her out the door. "As I thought, Eoghanan. Stay with the lass and help her once I lift the spell. When she's composed herself, both of ye come and find me. We will do the spell tonight."

I had one brief moment of confusion where I wondered why I would need help, then the spell lifted. Everything—my panic over my son being gone, my shock at watching Jeffrey disappear, my disbelief that apparently magic existed in the world, my worry over Eoghanan—it all hit me at once.

As Morna and Jerry left us, closing the door behind them, I collapsed into a fit of sobs.

CHAPTER 21

I didn't cry long. I couldn't allow myself to waste time that way when all I wanted to do was use Morna's hocus pocus to get my son back. I didn't want to cry at all, but as soon as she lifted the spell, I couldn't help it; the sudden rush of so many emotions sent me into a sort of mini-hysteria. I gasped and cried and screamed in quick succession.

I allowed myself five minutes of good, uncontrollable panic. Then I stood from the bed, swallowing all of it.

"Ok, I'm ready."

"Grace. . . " Eoghanan twisted me so I faced him. "I promise ye that he's safe."

"Don't." I wrenched from his grasp, knowing that if he tried to comfort me I'd start crying again. He looked as if I'd slapped him. I made haste to apologize, walking toward him and standing up on the tip of my toes, kissing him gently.

It was the only intimate act that had taken place between us since our first kiss. Rather than the raw heat that had flooded my body last time, the brush of his kiss calmed me, comforted me in a way I'd never experienced before. I realized in that instant that it didn't matter how little I knew about him, how short the time we'd known one another. Whatever this was between us, it was right.

"I'm sorry," I said, wrapping my arms around him, allowing my head to lean against his chest. "It's just, I'll lose it again if we talk about it. I don't understand any of this and it...it scares me." I let go and took half a step away from him. "Everything scares me right now. Cooper. Jeffrey. Morna. This..." I touched my chest and then his, and he grasped my hand, holding it in place against him.

"Ach, lass, I have never been so frightened in my life. I know ye canna understand all of this, not yet, but ye will when ye see it. I know ye canna help but worry about Cooper, but Morna wouldna let harm come to him and neither would my family. He and Jeffrey are both safe; I'd stake my life on it."

I nodded, sniffling as I tried to keep from crying again. "I just need him back."

"I know. Let's go to him, aye?"

I wanted to leave immediately, to let Morna spell me and send me hurtling back through time toward my son, but I couldn't get Eoghanan's wound off my mind.

"Eoghanan, Morna said that she'd slowly been building your strength to travel back, but that the time between now and your home was too far for you yet. What does that mean? It's your skin, isn't it? It's still not healed well enough."

"Aye, but I'll do my best to survive it. The first time Morna sent me back, she sent me to the park where I saw ye and Cooper. When she pulled me back here, my wound split open and bled verra badly."

"Yeah, I figured it was something like that. Nope. Sorry." I pulled away, opening the door and leaving to search for Morna. Eoghanan followed behind me. "There is no way I am letting you go back with me. The park wasn't that long ago. What do you think will happen to you if you're sent back multiple centuries?"

"I doona care. I willna allow ye to go without me." He grabbed my arm and spun me toward him, gripping me tightly.

"You won't allow me?"

"No, and Morna willna allow it, either."

Jerking away from him, I called for her. "Morna, I'm ready to go. Eoghanan is staying here."

"No. I willna do it, lass." He wasn't screaming like I was. He said it quietly, calmly, completely unflustered by the possibility of his imminent death.

"He's right. I willna spell ye back unless he goes with ye." Morna appeared suddenly in the hallway, spools of medicinal cloth in her arms.

"What if it kills him? What is all that for?"

Morna shook her head, clearly annoyed, and held them up for Eoghanan to see.

"Ye must think I am not a verra good witch. I willna let the lad die. Now. Come with me."

"How would I know what kind of witch you are? I didn't even know witches actually existed until today."

She ignored me, instead leading us into Eoghanan's room where she'd stripped the bed of its blankets, leaving only a sheet. "Eoghanan, strip yer clothes. I will bind ye up so that when the scar rips open, at least it will be held in place when ye come back together." She glanced over at me briefly. "Give him some privacy, unless ye wish to see every inch of him."

Eoghanan laughed, his eyes meeting mine. "Perhaps ye might want to step out just a moment."

***

*M*orna called me back inside nearly thirty minutes later. No matter how serious the situation, the sight of Eoghanan wrapped up like a mummy had Morna squirming with barely suppressed laughter.

"What's the matter with both of you?" I asked, frustrated with their behavior. "You don't even know if this is going to work."

Shaking her head, Morna said, "Doona worry, it will work. I've made a special salve to place upon the wound. As long as the bandages are not removed for a few days, it should do the trick. 'Tis something I could have done much earlier, but Eoghanan needed to remain here for a while longer, even if he dinna know it at the time."

I tilted my head to one side, studying her. "Why's that?" Everyone—Eoghanan, Cooper, Jeffrey—they all seemed to adore Morna. I wasn't quite there yet. She was too cryptic and had a penchant for meddling that had turned everything I thought I knew about the world, and my own life, upside down.

"If he'd left when he could've, he wouldna have met ye, lass. At least thank me for that, for whether ye are ready to say it yet or no, the two of ye are a fine match."

I couldn't very well argue with that. She was right, but I still felt awkward and shy. I fumbled for something else to say. "Why didn't you just stitch him up?"

"I am a witch, not a seamstress. I'm too squeamish to go about sewing him up from head to toe. Are ye ready?"

She didn't wait for me to answer, moving quickly on from the end of her question to muttering words I couldn't understand.

Eoghanan reached for my hand. I gladly took it as pain started to radiate throughout my body.

"Doona let go, lass. 'Twill all be over soon."

CHAPTER 22

*M*cMillan Castle—*1647*

"*M*ooommmm....Moooommmm..."

Some part of my brain registered the word, drawn out each time, as if in a song. My head ached something dreadful, and I couldn't remember what I'd been doing an hour ago or where I was now.

I racked my brain for the answer. When it came to me, I threw myself forward, opening my eyes as my son pounced on me, wrapping his little arms around my neck. "Cooper!" The movement jarred my head. With my arms still securely around him, I grabbed my forehead, willing the throbbing to stop.

I went still at the sound of an unfamiliar male voice. "Aye, I havena experienced it myself, but my wife says the ache in yer head is the worst part. At least ye dinna land in the pond." I opened my eyes to see a man slightly taller than Eoghanan standing in front of me. He wore a kilt and had dark hair and brooding eyes.

Eoghanan sat up next to me. Blood seeped through the cloth wound around him. "I doona wish to argue with ye, but 'tis not my head that hurts."

I shifted, swinging Cooper's weight onto my side so I could lean over and check on Eoghanan. "You are a stupid, stupid man. You should not have come."

"'Tis not nearly as bad as I expected, lass. Morna said it might bleed a little."

He struggled to stand, and the tall man reached out a hand to assist him. Once he was standing, I could see he was right; he only bled a little.

My nerves relaxed and I stood up, Cooper still clinging to my hip.

"Are you okay?" I reached up and brushed my son's hair back, examining his head for apparent injury, just like every mom in every TV movie did when she found her missing child. I realized it was a pointless gesture and stopped, settling instead for planting a big kiss on the top of his head.

.

"Yeah, Mom, I'm awesome! Everything is lit by candles here, and I got to pee in a bucket! Even the bathtub is just a big old bucket that they carry into your room. I only wish they had dragons. I really thought there would be some here." His voice drifted a little as he reflected on his disappointment.

I heard footsteps approaching and another voice joined the conversation. I turned to see Jeffrey walking along with a stunning redhead by his side. Her belly was swollen, and I guessed her to be in the last stages of pregnancy. I hurried to Jeffrey and hugged him tightly.

"You must be Grace. I'm Mitsy," the woman said. She extended a hand. I took it, and she continued, "I have some ibuprofen for your head that should help. I know it's got to be hurting you. The time traveling thing is a tough one."

The man who stood next to Eoghanan, the man whose name I

still didn't know, reached over to grab Mitsy's hand, pulling her into him.

"Um...so you have ibuprofen?" I asked.

Mitsy laughed, nodding excitedly. "Yes, Morna often sends modern-ish things to Conall Castle for Bri, and I grabbed some the last time I was there."

"Oh." I didn't know who Bri was, but I didn't ask.

"Grace." Eoghanan stepped closer to me, placing a hand on the small of my back. "This is my brother, Baodan. He is laird here at McMillan Castle, and ye have already met Mitsy, for she has better manners and has already introduced herself."

Mitsy laughed and threw her arms around Eoghanan. She clung to him, despite his bandages, and he gladly embraced her. I could sense the strong friendship between them. I expected that their relationship was part of the reason he'd not questioned my relationship with Jeffrey once he'd calmed down and allowed me to explain it to him.

"I'm so glad you're back, E-o." Her voice was soft and near cracking, but she held back her tears.

She'd called him E-o, just like Cooper, and I realized that Mitsy was the beloved 'girlfriend' he'd mentioned. I really needed to teach him the definition of that word.

"I've been so worried about you. I mean, I trusted Morna to take care of you, but...I still can't believe you did that. You're a stupid, stupid man."

Eoghanan laughed loudly, prying Mitsy off of him. "I doona think I like that word. I've been called it too many times today."

"What did he do?" My question seemed to interrupt their moment a little, but I wanted to know. In this time, a sword injury made much more sense, but Eoghanan's previous description of the event had been much too vague.

Mitsy gave Eoghanan a look that said she was surprised I didn't already know. "Their brother was a crazy sociopath who murdered anyone who inconvenienced him. He tried to do the same to me, but Eoghanan jumped in the way of the sword. Then I killed the monster."

"Oh." I was saying that word a lot lately. She'd explained what had happened to wound Eoghanan only a fraction better than he had, and it did nothing to satisfy my curiosity. I looked over at him, deciding that further probing could wait. He'd wilted a bit and now stood leaning heavily onto his left foot. He looked like he might fall over at any moment.

Cooper must have noticed the same thing, and he squirmed in my arms so I would set him down. He ran to Eoghanan's side, leaning against his left leg as if trying to prop him up. "Hey, you don't look so good, E-o. You all right?"

Eoghanan placed a hand on top of Cooper's head. He tried to smile at him, but no light reached his eyes. He started to grow paler with each passing second.

"I'm verra tired. I think we should go inside. Baodan, would ye help me to my chambers?"

Baodan was at his side in an instant, propping him up against his shoulder. Baodan smiled back at his wife—a silent conversation where I was sure he'd asked her to see to the rest of us.

Once Baodan and Eoghanan were inside the castle, Mitsy said, "You're lucky you got an explanation about what was happening before you showed up here. Jeffrey had a bit of a meltdown."

"I did not." He attempted to argue, but his eyes were still glazed over with lingering shock.

Mitsy nodded. *"Definite meltdown."* She mouthed the words silently to me, smiling. "Anyway, once we got him settled down, he and Cooper spent most of the night exploring the place. I think they'll be fine if we leave them on their own. I'm in desperate need of some modern-day girl talk."

CHAPTER 23

"Hey, stranger." Three days after we'd arrived, I stepped inside Eoghanan's chamber for the first time. I'd kept my distance until now, hoping that without a distraction, he'd be more apt to stay in bed and rest.

At least, this is the reason I told myself so I wouldn't feel guilty. Truthfully, I'd taken advantage of his need to rest to give myself time to think.

All of it was true—the fact that Morna was a witch, her ability to send those she wished hurtling through time—I could no longer deny any of it. And now, I had to accept what that meant.

Nothing more could ever happen between Eoghanan and me.

I'd hoped that a few days away from him would allow me to gain some perspective. That after wandering around the castle and observing all of the strange differences between this time and my own that I would feel out of place and ready to return home.

I didn't feel that way at all.

I loved it here—the simplicity, the inaccessibility of it. I knew if it was only myself I had to worry about, I could stay here forever. All of the people at the castle, including Eoghanan's family members, could not have been more warm and kind.

Accustomed to strange, time-traveling Americans due to Mitsy and Bri—who I'd yet to meet—we'd settled in quite nicely .

Cooper seemed to love it here, as well. He used the castle as a sort of massive playground, determined to discover every secret nook and passageway. Jeffrey, I thought, looked at it as a vacation. After years of working the grind at a law firm, he reveled in being able to do what he considered "manly" tasks like horseback riding and learning how to shoot a bow and arrow.

Still, it was easy for them to enjoy the changes for a short amount of time, an impossibility to ask them to do so forever.

I'd set my mind to speaking to Eoghanan about this, to explaining to him that the three of us would need to return home soon. After walking into his room and greeting him, I took in the droopy, glazed, plastered look on his face.

"Grace, lass." He said my name slowly. He was drunk. I could tell by his droopy eyes, but he wasn't so drunk that he'd lost concern for his own behavior. He didn't want me to know that he was drunk.

"I apologize for this, lass. 'Tis my own doing, not his."

It was Baodan's voice, and I turned toward it. "Why?"

"'Tis time to remove his bandages, but the blood has dried the cloth to him. When I went to remove the bandages from the side of his face..." He paused. "I doona think he screamed like that when the blade tore through him. I thought it best to give him something to dull the pain so the rest of the removal might go easier on him."

"Ah, good idea. Do you need me to leave? I can come back later."

"No, doona leave, Grace." Eoghanan called to me, swinging his feet over the side of the bed and trying to stand. "I'd like for ye to remove them from me."

Baodan gave me no chance to answer him, moving across the room to push his brother back down on the bed. "Ye doona truly wish that lad. When ye are sober, ye will regret asking it of her."

Eoghanan persisted. "Aye, I do wish it. I am not all that drunk, Baodan. Now, leave us be."

Baodan retreated from Eoghanan's side, but lingered in front of me a moment, a question in his eyes.

"I don't mind. Really, we'll be fine."

Nodding once, Baodan left, closing the door behind him. As I walked toward Eoghanan, he smiled a lazy smile that made my insides flutter. I'd yet to see such an unrestrained grin from him. He usually thought too much to appear this relaxed. It was an incredibly endearing look.

I had a sneaking suspicion the conversation I needed to have with him wouldn't happen today.

"Are you sure you want me to do this? I'm not really qualified. I'm not a witch or a nurse, so..."

I now stood next to his bed, and he reached up and pulled me down so that I sat on the edge. "Aye, lass. Yer hands will be far more gentle than my brother's."

"Okay." I ran my fingertips over the exposed scar that ran down the side of his face. Whatever Morna had placed upon it had altered the skin completely. Only days before the line had been red, angry, relatively new. Now its shade was a close match to the rest of his skin and had the look of a much older scar. It had healed as much as it ever would. "It looks so much better, Eoghanan."

"Aye?"

I couldn't tell if he'd heard a word I said. His eyes were closed, and he was enjoying the feel of my fingertips as they trailed his face. When they reached the base of his neck where the remaining wrap started, he grabbed my hand, bringing it up to his lips, and kissed my palm.

"I love yer hands, lass, and the way ye make me feel when ye touch me. Do ye remember when ye cut my hair?" His words were slow, slightly slurred, and incredibly affecting.

"Yes, I do. What about it?"

He still gripped my hand. "All I could think of was yer touch and how it made me feel. I wanted −"

"Okay..." I jerked away, standing up as fast as I could, doing a strange little dance where I shook out my hands and hopped from foot to foot to clear my head. "I think maybe you are further into the bottle than you think, mister."

He smiled, getting up from the bed so that he stood in front of me, smiling that same lazy grin. "Aye, mayhap so, Grace, though every word I spoke and was about to speak is the truth."

I took a calming breath, preparing myself for the task ahead. After what he'd just told me, I was unsettled at the thought of the somewhat intimate act . . . the two of us so close, my hands touching him again. My heart fluttered like hummingbird wings. How was it possible that he could stir such ambivalence in me with just a few words? Feelings of both longing and wariness coursed through me, but I was determined to follow through with what I'd said I would do.

"Are you ready to get started?" I didn't allow him the chance to answer. Gripping the top of the fabric near his neck, I tugged to test out just how tightly it was bound. "Does that hurt?"

"No, not in the way that my face did."

I nodded, continuing to pull at the bandage, "Good. I'm going to keep going then."

He said nothing. For the following minutes I worked quietly, pulling and then reaching around him to gather the fabric, repeating the motion over and over again. He didn't scream, didn't wince; he simply watched me so intently that an evident tension began to build around us in the room. Each time I leaned forward to unwind the cloth around his back, I was tempted to linger.

I wanted nothing more than for him to stop me, hold me in his arms, kiss me again, but my rational mind told me to keep to my work. No matter how much I wanted to tell that voice in my head to go hang, I inevitably had to leave here; it would be foolish to complicate things further.

"Where have ye been, Grace?"

The question caught me off guard. Despite the fact that I feigned ignorance, I knew exactly what he meant. "What do you mean? I've been right here."

"No, ye have been anywhere but right here, lass. Ye have plans to leave."

He didn't ask it as a question, and his keen observation caused my hand to still for a brief moment. I'd unwound the cloth to the bottom of his waist. All that was left was his right leg, but I hesitated to go further.

"I..." I couldn't very well lie to him. Of course I had plans to leave. "I don't really have a choice. There's only a few more days before I'm due back in New York."

"New York. Do ye mean for yer article?" He reached behind himself to grab the roll of bandages I held. "Put them down, lass. Look at me." I met his gaze. "Yer magazine will receive the money promised to them with or without yer article. The mysterious benefactor...I believe 'twas Jerry."

Of course it was. "How do you know about that?"

"The telephone was right outside my bedchamber. I heard him speaking to yer boss, though I dinna understand it until the evening when ye told me about yer job."

The telephone. I had a sudden flashback to my phone conversation with my sister and the noise I thought I'd heard behind his door. "The telephone...you heard me, huh?"

He smiled, reaching up with his right hand to tuck some hair behind my ear. The movement in his shoulder was much improved. "Aye, though I could only hear ye, not whoever ye spoke with."

"My sister."

He nodded. "I thought as much." Smiling with one half of his mouth, he released my arms, pulled the blanket across his lower body. Slipping his hands beneath it, he began unwrapping his lower waist and leg.

In a matter of moments he was finished. He reached for my hand and I sat beside him, looking at him with sympathy. He held his liquor relatively well, but he'd not feel well tomorrow.

"How does it feel? The scar?" I asked.

"I feel like myself for the first time since it happened. I canna believe Morna allowed me to lay there for so long when she could have healed it in a couple of days; though I know now why she did."

That look in his eyes was back—the same look that would not have shown itself so boldly had he been sober.

"Why's that?"

"Why do ye think, lass?" He kissed me, a consuming kiss so different from what I'd expect from him.

It took some effort on my part, but I managed to draw back a scant inch. "Eoghanan." His name came breathless on my lips.

"Hush, Grace."

He slipped one hand behind my head, pressing our mouths together in a kiss so deep I thought I might drown in it, completely lose myself. I knew what he wanted—I wanted it, too. But I was leaving his time soon, going back to mine, and so I hesitated.

Eoghanan must've sensed or felt my hesitation. He let out one long, shaky breath and paused, resting his forehead on mine. "I couldna want ye more, lass," he said, then gave me one more brief kiss and scooted away. "I respect ye too much to do something that ye might regret, Grace. If we were to love each other now, I would not be able to let ye leave, and ye have said that ye must."

CHAPTER 24

Mitsy kicked off her shoes and allowed her feet to sink into the pond water, sighing as it soothed her pregnancy-swollen feet. I could remember exactly how she felt.

"Oh, that's nice. That's really nice." She sighed. "I know it seems like you've got a big decision to make, Grace, but can I let you in on a secret?"

I sat with my legs dangling in the pond, as well, leaning back on my hands as I watched Cooper making a mud pie along the shore. "Sure, shoot," I replied, in answer to her question.

The bottom hem of her dress dropped into the water. "Oh, no! These dresses . . ." She huffed a frustrated breath. "Usually they're not that bad, but now I just want to live in a pair of yoga pants until this baby decides to drop out of me."

I laughed, patting her arm in sympathy. "I understand."

She waved a hand in dismissal. "Anyhow, back to what I was saying. Don't battle it."

"I'm sorry. I don't know what you mean."

"I think you know exactly what I mean." She smiled.

Mitsy wasn't the type of person I would have pegged as being intuitive. I liked her immensely, but it surprised me that she'd been able to so easily figure out what I stewed over.

"Was it easy for you?" I asked. "Deciding to stay here?"

"Yes. Not right away, I guess. But as soon as I realized that everyone that I loved was here, there was nothing else left for me back home. Modern conveniences meant nothing compared to all of that."

"But I do have people that I love who aren't here. Jeffrey, Cooper, Bebop." She didn't realize that it wasn't a battle over whether to stay or go. I knew I couldn't stay here. I simply fought a war with myself trying to accept that.

"I don't know who Bebop is, but Jeffrey and Cooper are right here with you, and as far as I can see, they look very happy."

They did, but we'd only been here a few days. How would Cooper feel in a few months when he couldn't go out and buy any more dinosaur toys? What kind of mood would Jeffrey be in come football season when there was no television?

"Sure, but that's because neither one of them expects to stay here."

"How do you know that? Jeffrey would do anything for you. I've only known the man a few days, but I can see that."

I shrugged. That was precisely the problem. Jeffrey's whole life had been a series of sacrifices he'd made for me. I couldn't ask him for anything else. I wouldn't. "Believe me, I know that if I asked Jeffrey to do so, he would. It's the very reason I will never ask it of him."

"Let me ask you something."

Mitsy was incredibly direct. I appreciated it. Her honesty was refreshing, and it made it impossible to feel like a stranger in her presence.

"If you weren't worried about Cooper and Jeffrey, would you stay? At least for a while?"

I nodded, but then caught myself. "Yes. I mean, if Eoghanan wanted me to, but he's not asked me. Not directly."

Mitsy laughed. "Eoghanan wouldn't. As far as men go, he's one of the best communicators I've ever seen. He's thoughtful and attentive, but he's incredibly self-sacrificing. He would never ask anything if he thought it selfish. Did he not tell you anything about what happened to him?"

"Not much more than what you mentioned the other day."

"I know. I was vague on purpose. I didn't want to go into the whole story in front of him. Eoghanan would have tried to downplay it, and his actions were too noteworthy for that."

"What happened?" I lifted my weight off of my arms, stretching and twisting my wrists so that I could settle in to finally hear the story I'd been waiting for.

"Baodan was married to someone before me. Her name was Osla, and she died very early on in their marriage. That was over seven years ago, and from the time of her death until right before Eoghanan's injury, Baodan believed Eoghanan responsible."

"Why?" It was a notion almost more difficult for me to believe than learning that witches and time travel existed.

"Baodan and Eoghanan had another brother, Niall, a lousy scumbag who manipulated everyone in their family for years."

She continued, explaining what Eoghanan had done for Osla during her life and then for Baodan after her death, sacrificing his relationship with his brother to keep from hurting him. Then, how he'd saved Mitsy by stepping in front of Niall's blade, protecting both her and her unborn child.

"He's the rarest of men, Grace. He will do anything for the people he loves, even let them go if he thinks that's what they need. He would never ask you to stay, but it will break his heart if you leave. Nobody else is going to tell you that, but I will. He loves you, even if he doesn't know that yet; even if he hasn't said it to you, he does. And you love him, no matter the length of time that you've known him. Morna would not have sent you here otherwise. Believe me. She's that good."

I watched as she pulled her feet out of the water and stood, readying herself to take her leave.

"And you know what else?" Mitsy added, as if it were an afterthought, "She wouldn't have let Cooper and Jeffrey wind up back here unless they were meant to be here as well. Just something to think about. I'll catch you later." She started the short walk back to the castle. "I have to pee again. I have to pee all the time now. Literally, like twenty times a day."

"Hey, Coop. Can I sit with ya a minute?" asked Jeffrey.

Cooper smiled and nodded, still facing the pond. It was his dad's voice; he'd know it anywhere. "'Course you can. You know you don't have to ask me. You're the dad, ya know?"

"I know, but sometimes a man needs his space. I didn't want to interrupt you if you needed some thinkin' time."

A man...he liked the way that sounded. He wasn't a man yet, but as soon as he lost all of his baby teeth, he would be. Only a few more years to go. "No, I wasn't thinkin.' I was just watching the sky and making this mud pie." He held up his muddy fingers. "I do my thinking in the mornings."

"Right. My early bird. What have you been thinking lately?"

Cooper took a breath, trying to remember everything. He thought about so many things, surely his dad didn't expect him to list each one. "About what?"

"About this place. What do you think about it? Are you ready to go home soon?"

Home? Out of all the things that he'd thought about, home wasn't one of them. He liked it here too much to think about home. "No, I'm not ready to go home, Dad. We don't have to right away, do we?"

His dad rubbed his back a little. "No, son. I was just seeing if you were homesick."

"I only get homesick when I'm not with you and Mom." That wasn't completely true. "And when I don't have my bag of dinosaurs, but guess what, Dad?"

"What?"

"Bao...Baoghan...Baodan. Umm...I think I'm gonna have to come up with a nickname for him too—like I did E-o. Anyway, that guy," he pointed in the direction of the castle so his dad would know who he was talking about, "he brought me my bag this morning. He said it just appeared on the doorstep. I guess that old witch sent it back for me. Now I won't ever be homesick. I have everything I need." Everything he needed not to be homesick, but he still missed one thing. "What about you, Dad? Are you homesick?"

Dad scooted closer to him, pulling him into his lap. "Nope. I'm the same way. As long as I'm with you and your mother, I'm all set. There's only one thing that would make it extra cool."

Cooper knew right away what his dad was talking about, and he nodded. "Bebop."

"Yep. Bebop would love it here."

"Yeah, he would. Dad, do you think we could get Bebop here? That way we wouldn't ever have to leave."

"I don't know, Coop. Maybe. But that is sort of what I wanted to talk to you about. Do you see your Mom over there?"

Of course he saw her. He'd been watching her sad face all day. She didn't want to leave here, either. "Yeah, she's sad. She doesn't want to leave E-o, but she feels like she has to. For us."

Jeffrey kissed him on his head, messing with his hair, bouncing around his curls. "You are such a smart kid, Coop."

"If I don't want to leave, and you don't want to leave, then Mom doesn't need to feel like she has to, either. We could all just stay."

Dad stood suddenly, smiling down at him. "My thoughts exactly, Coop. My thoughts exactly."

$\mathcal{D}$inner consisted of a meaty and delicious stew served with a loaf of bread that, while tasty, was hard enough to serve as a weapon should the need arise. I'd hoped to retire early, not to sleep, but just to seek some time alone. I seemed to be needing a lot of that lately—to think and perhaps sulk a while. It didn't happen.

I walked a half dozen steps out of the dining hall before Kenna McMillan stopped me. Eoghanan's mother was a stunning woman who showed only the slightest signs of aging, with a few perfectly-placed strands of hair turning gray. On her, it was rather fetching.

She was also one of the most kind and open-minded women I'd ever met. Mitsy's blunt way of speaking and no-nonsense attitude came as no surprise; she was born in the twenty-first century, after all. But, Kenna rivaled her.

I'd expected a woman born so many centuries earlier, in a time when women were often thought of in a very different way, to be more reserved in her speech, more judgmental of situations that differed from societal expectations, perhaps. Kenna was none of these things.

She'd opened her son's home and her arms to my family, never questioning the odd situation, never making us feel unwelcome or less-than. She said exactly what she thought and took bull from no one. I hoped that if I spent more time around her and Mitsy some of that attitude might rub off on me.

"Grace, do ye have a moment?"

I slowed my pace, allowing her to catch up to me. She quickly looped an arm with mine and deftly steered me in the opposite direction.

"I verra much wish that...what is it that Mitsy has called it? Email? I wish the invention of such a thing could arise now and not hundreds of years after I'm dead."

I laughed, patting her hand sympathetically as she walked me out the back door of the castle and into the garden. "News travel too slow for you? I have to admit, I'm enjoying the break from it all. It's nice not to be so connected, to know that people can't reach you every second of every day."

Kenna nodded. "Aye, I wouldna want to be that available, perhaps, but I can see how it would be verra helpful when guests are arriving. They could send news of their arrival more than just the morning before."

"Are you expecting guests?"

"Aye, the Conalls are coming to stay with us until the arrival of Mitsy's babe. They sent a messenger some three days before they were to arrive here, but the man fell ill and just arrived today."

"Oh. Well, what can I help you with?"

She shook her head, laughing, "Oh, not a thing, dear. 'Tis only that the bedchamber ye are staying in...I'm afraid we willna have enough rooms for everyone if ye stay in it alone."

"Oh." For a moment, I wondered if she meant to ask us to leave, but she quickly continued to clarify.

"Now, doona think I'm giving ye an opportunity to slip away from here, for not one of us wants that. 'Tis only we must find some other room to place ye."

I took a deep breath, relaxing the sudden anxiety that had built up. I was glad she wasn't ready for me to leave. I wasn't ready to, either, no matter how much I knew I needed to.

"I'll just stay with Cooper and Jeffrey. It will be no problem. I can sleep on the floor, or Jeffrey can."

Kenna regarded me as if I'd just suggested we run the length of the garden completely naked. "Sleep on the floor? No. I'll enter my grave before I have a guest in my," she corrected herself, "my son's home, sleep on the floor."

She made the correction because, technically, it was correct. But I didn't believe for a second that she was any less hands-on in the running of the castle than she was before her husband's death. Mitsy had mentioned to me, when she'd told me Eoghanan's story, how Kenna had been so ill for so long, reduced nearly to death. Standing before this strong, beautiful, headstrong woman now, I couldn't begin to picture it.

"Well," I started, "I'm sure this isn't customary, but I don't think Mitsy would mind. I could stay with Mitsy and..." I felt incredibly uncomfortable making a suggestion about how things should be done, but it seemed to me as if she wanted my help in finding a solution. "Baodan could move in with Eoghanan for a few nights."

She stopped walking and faced me, gathering up both of my hands in hers. "No, that wouldna be customary. Neither is what I am going to suggest, but it seems I will have to help ye on, since ye willna make the suggestion yerself. I willna ask my son to spend the night without his pregnant wife, nor she without him."

She fumbled with my hands a bit, hesitating. I could tell the exact moment she decided to get on with what she meant to say. She straightened, looked me in the eyes, and the corner of her mouth pulled up a bit into a knowing smile.

"Ye will stay with Eoghanan."

My eyes widened. She laughed before I could respond, releasing her grip on my hands and walking hastily back into the castle before I could argue, leaving me standing alone in the garden with my mouth hanging slightly open.

She was a modern woman indeed. If there'd ever been a woman born out of her true time, it was Kenna McMillan.

"What are you doing, Grace?"

I messed around the bedchamber I'd been placed in originally, doing my best to waste as much time as possible before I went to invite myself into Eoghanan's room. I'd been pretending to tidy things up, but the room was immaculate so I suspected I looked a bit mad, flittering about the room, lifting objects as I brushed away at nothing with my hand. Jeffrey's question confirmed my suspicions.

"Uh, hey, I was just..." I gave up. "I don't know what I'm doing. What's up?"

He smiled and stepped inside, moving to place an arm around me, pulling me in close.

"Who would have thought, huh? All of this. . ." he motioned to the room with his free hand. "It's crazy, but kind of wonderful, too. Coop really loves it here."

I nodded, gladly leaning into Jeffrey's comforting arm. "Yes, I'm sure he does for a few days, but he'll be ready to get home soon."

"I wouldn't be so sure, Grace. He's an odd kid; I kind of think this place suits him even better than back home."

I couldn't imagine what he was getting at, but I wished he'd stop. Believing that there was a possibility that Cooper could be happy here made me hope for something I couldn't have. "Well, there's a lot more to it than just Cooper's happiness."

Jeffrey squeezed my shoulder and kissed the side of my temple, rubbing my back sympathetically. "Are you saying that you wouldn't be happy here?"

I shook my head against his chest. "No. I think I would."

"So what's there to think about, Grace? Let's stay. What have you got to lose? It's not a prison here. Mitsy and Baodan have both said that should you ever want to leave, should you ever need to return home, Morna would help you." He released me and paced around the room. "If you leave now, though, you'll regret it, Grace. You'll wonder forever if you missed out on the real thing. The thing you're never gonna get from me, the thing you want Cooper to see exists."

Of course he would give me permission to stay. I'd expect nothing less from him, which is why I'd hoped he wouldn't realize how much I wanted to stay. I'd been a fool to think I could hide anything from him.

"Jeffrey, you don't want to be here. Are you saying that you'll leave? Because you won't. I know you wouldn't leave Cooper here, and I am not going to ask you to do that for me."

"You're not asking me, Grace. I'm telling you that I like it here, too. I'd like it anywhere as long as I have you and Cooper."

"No, we're not going to sacrifice Cooper's childhood, your job, your life, just because of this." I didn't even know what 'this' was. "This thing with Eoghanan."

"His childhood?" Jeffrey's voice was quickly growing frustrated. "A childhood of what? Seeing his mother unhappy because she sacrificed what she really wanted to give him what she *thought* he needed. A childhood of being picked on because he's smarter than all the other kids in his class and he'd rather read a book than play a video game?"

Jeffrey had made his point. I was using Cooper as an excuse. "Fine." Tears started to fill my eyes, and my voice cracked as I spoke. "It's not about Cooper. It's about you and how guilty I feel that every decision in your life has been about me. And...it's about Eoghanan. What if he doesn't even want me?"

He stormed past me, stopping in the doorway. "What a load of baloney, Grace. The man wouldn't spend half his days writing about you if he didn't want you. You're scared, and you need to grow up. You can only use being a mother as an excuse not to have your own life for so long."

The shock on my face must have been evident, for he nodded, continuing, "That's right, Grace. The man is crazy about you. I was playing with Cooper last night, and we stumbled across some old room where he writes. You should see it, Grace. Only a total idiot would turn down someone that thinks that highly of them. There are few men that could ever be worthy of you as far as I'm concerned, but he's one of them. Do not be an idiot."

He stepped out into the hallway.

"And you know what? My mind is made up, anyway. Even if you decide to leave, I'm staying right here."

It took some hunting, but shortly after Jeffrey left me, I went in search of the room he had mentioned that contained Eoghanan's writings.

It was filled with books, all neatly organized amongst cleanly-kept shelves, with candles ready to be lit lining the walls.

I moved slowly, setting it alight, taking in the beautiful cave-like atmosphere. It would have been a nice place to work on my article, which now would remain eternally unfinished.

Jeffrey didn't make idle threats or promises. If he said he'd made up his mind to stay, he would stay. And so would I.

In the middle of the room was a large table, and right in the center lay the open-faced journal. Eoghanan must have truly thought the room hidden to have left it out so blatantly. It was wrong of me to be here, to delve into his private thoughts without permission, but curiosity overtook me. I truly had no right to shame Cooper for eavesdropping. He came by it honestly.

The journal was new, not only the entries, but the binding itself was modern. It was the sort of special journal I could've ordered from a craftsman; the outside leather, the pages made of the highest quality paper, all sewn in thick gold-colored threads. It had the look of something old, but the date embossed on the inside flap of leather showed the date of its creation—two thousand and fourteen. I imagined it had arrived at the doorstep via Morna, right alongside my son's dinosaurs.

I thumbed through it, running my fingers over the ink-dried pages without really looking at the words, trying to work up the nerve to actually read them. When I finally did, I found myself taken aback. He'd not written so much about me, as for me.

"Do ye remember the day ye spent with Cooper in the park? I only know the lad's name for 'tis what ye called him when ye spoke. Ye have the loveliest voice I've ever heard."

I could think of few things less lovely than the sound of my voice. I cringed every time I heard it on any sort of home movie or recording.

"If ye ever read this, 'twill be many moons from now, but for me, 'twas just this afternoon. My body is bleeding and wounded from the journey, and I write with pages so far from my eyes I canna see them, but I must write every piece of ye down lest I forget ye. 'Twould break my heart to not remember every instant that I saw."

I put a finger on the page to hold my place and skipped forward a handful of pages, smiling as I did so. He'd told the truth about the page being far from his eyes. The page I read now was scribbled messily, the lines and words crooked with the effort it took him to hold the pen and move his fingers.

As his shoulder slowly healed, so did the neatness of his handwriting. It came as no surprise that in full form, with the complete movement of his shoulder restored, his last entry showed handwriting that was shockingly straight and neat.

I returned to where I'd left off reading.

"I have not ever been so frightened in my life as when I woke inside the park. The tall stone structures and the deafening noise were enough to make a man mad. My head and heart pounded as I struggled to understand the sights around me, and then my eyes found ye and the wee lad. Yer long blonde hair blew with the breeze, and ye laughed as ye pushed the boy on a strange seat that sent him flying in the air. Ye wore the breeches of a man, though I've never seen a man wear something so tight. God help me, lass, I couldna keep my eyes off ye. I couldna believe when I looked around and saw many lassies dressed such. Ye wore such lovely colors, the greens and blues in yer garments making yer eyes sparkle in the sun. I doona even know yer name, but my only dream tonight, should sleep find me, is that I should get to see yer face once again."

I closed my eyes as I reached the end of the entry, my fingers lingering lovingly on the last line. I remembered so little about that day. To have him detail it so attentively made it seem as if he'd started caring for me the first day he'd ever seen me. The adoration in his words was overwhelming. I flipped forward, finding an entry dated the day Cooper and I arrived at the inn.

"God, my heart stopped beating when I saw ye standing in the kitchen. To see ye when ye canna see me is one thing; to know that ye are looking back at me is another. I have not ever felt such a way before, lass. There is something between us, aye? I know that we doona know each other, but a feeling tells me I canna go back to a life before I met ye. I think 'tis how it should be, perhaps. I wouldna know, 'tis a verra new experience for me. I knew there was a reason my travels back sent me to ye. I dinna believe Morna when she said 'twas not her doing. It was, and I couldna be more grateful for it. I am verra fond of ye, lass. I think in time, ye will be of me, as well."

I'd been too shocked at Cooper's exclamations of knowing the man to let it sink in at the time, but I'd felt much the same way. A sudden shift in my being, like a gear in my brain clicking into place when I saw him. From that moment, I couldn't be in the same room with him without being intensely aware of him every moment, without feeling his presence deep in my bones.

"I knew the wee lad had seen me, but I'd hoped it hadna been so clearly that he'd recognize me. I hope that the idea dinna scare ye, lass. I saw yer eyes widen at Cooper's exclamation and, aye, I suppose 'tis a bit unsettling to think that I might have been watching ye without yer knowledge. And although I have, 'tis been nothing but care and admiration in my heart while doin' so."

I had no doubt about that. As he'd said, Morna controlled where he went, not him. Cooper had known that as well. From his first glimpse of Eoghanan in the airport, when he'd tried to tell me about him and I'd been frightened, he'd said he could see what a good man he was from his eyes.

There were several more entries that I skimmed, coming finally to the last one, written only this morning.

"I am a man who has denied myself many things, but none has been so difficult as denying myself ye. To know that ye plan to leave here 'tis not something I wish to think about. I understand why ye feel that ye must, but ye are wrong. Ye belong here. Ye and Cooper and Jeffrey, ye could all be a part of this family. I need ye. I love ye, lass. Doona leave."

Mitsy was right. He cared too much about others and too little about himself to ask me what he wanted outside of these journals. What a gift, though he'd not wished for me to see it, to know how he felt; to know that he'd not slowly warmed to me, but opened his heart to me so immediately, trusting so much more readily than I had that some things are meant to be.

I closed the journal, my eyes brimming with tears and abundant gratitude for this strange, miraculous change in the path of my life.

I heard sudden footsteps behind me. I knew it was Eoghanan even before I turned.

"I've been looking everywhere for ye, lass."

CHAPTER 27

"I'm sorry. I shouldn't have..." Standing, I faced Eoghanan, waiting for him to approach me. Truthfully, I was only sorry that I'd been caught; I didn't regret having read the journal.

When he reached me, he cupped either side of my face, brushing away a loose tear with his thumb before kissing me gently. I relaxed against him, matching his slow kisses with my own.

After a moment, he pulled away and leaned in to whisper in my ear. "Doona be sorry. They were meant for ye, only, mayhap, not so soon."

I wound one of my hands into his hair, holding him close to me. "It's not too soon. I'm not going anywhere. You can thank Jeffrey for helping me see that I couldn't."

"Aye, I shall thank him, lass, but not tonight." He kissed me again, but not slowly like before; it was deeper, more urgent, and I molded my body against him, my knees growing weak with anticipation.

A sudden commotion sounded below us, the voices of many people echoing up through the stairwell. Disappointed, I groaned internally, pulling away from his kiss and allowing my head to drop onto his shoulder. "Your guests are here."

"Guests?" He lifted my head, asking for more explanation.

"Yes, the Conalls are here, I think. They've come to stay until the baby is born."

He nodded. "I am not surprised." Gripping my hand, he pulled me out of the room and started moving down the stairwell rather quickly.

I assumed he was taking me to greet them, but as he turned the corner leading to his bedchamber rather than continuing to the great hall, I smiled. "Where are we going?"

"To my chambers, Grace. Ye can meet them in the morning. What I have to say to you must be said in private."

Something in the tone of his voice spiraled a quiver of warmth through me. If we'd not been moving, I knew my knees would have actually buckled. I'd always thought that a dramatic cliché, but it wasn't—not with Eoghanan—not now. His words thrilled me so much that my heart sped up to a frightening pace. I could scarcely breathe. All of the blood seemed to drain from my brain, leaving no other thoughts but him and what I anticipated the night ahead promised the two of us.

***

He'd been a fool to let her leave his chambers the evening before without speaking his heart. He should have begged her to stay. He was finished behaving as a fool.

It was the part of himself he hated most—his desire to always do what he thought right. In that moment of cowardice, he'd believed it right of him to let her go if she thought it best. But he'd realized his mistake the moment she'd left his room. There was nothing right about his life without Grace in it.

How many times had his notions of right or wrong been

misguided? All that had happened with Osla, Niall, and Baodan should have shown him that. Sometimes he made very bad mistakes. Letting her believe he didn't want her here, even for a moment, was one of them.

He needed her in a way he had never needed anyone else. He needed her and Cooper to show him that he could be the man he knew he was, not the man others had believed him to be for so many years.

And Grace needed him.

Eoghanan knew he could help her open up to believing that being a mother didn't negate her need to be desired or loved. Each time he kissed her, he could sense her restraint. Even now, as he opened his bedchamber door, he sensed a sudden restraint in her. Too many years alone had somehow convinced the lass that after motherhood, her own desires no longer mattered. It was the one foolish notion he'd seen in her.

Mothers in loving relationships with the man in their lives made the happiest moms; just as fathers who found joy in their wives were the happiest of men.

He would prove that to her tonight.

The moment after Eoghanan's bedchamber door closed, we were in each other's arms. He kissed me gently, but he must have sensed my hesitation for he stopped abruptly. He kept our bodies pressed together and he cupped my head in his hands. "Where are ye, lass? For 'tis not right here with me."

I closed my eyes in resignation of how right he was. I wanted nothing more than to be present in this moment, to enjoy him in every imaginable way, but something inside of me resisted. "Coop, he..."

Eoghanan didn't allow me to finish. Covering my mouth with one of his palms, he said, "Hush, Grace. This night is not about

Cooper, nor Jeffrey, nor anyone else within these walls. Ye needn't worry about him. He's with his dad and our new guests, one of whom I know has him up in her lap talking all about his wee dinosaurs. Bri loves children. Even if ye were with Cooper now, she will be the one who has his attention.

I knew he was right, and a part of me was desperate for him to kiss me senseless. But another part of me felt guilty for being so self-indulgent.

As far as I could see, motherhood was the greatest blessing one could receive in life, but with it came a sort of constant, eternal sense of guilt I'd yet to learn how to shake. I'd spent much of my childhood alone, under the care of nannies or Jeffrey's father, and I remembered wondering why my parents didn't want to spend time with me. What was so important that they were always gone?

I didn't ever want Cooper to wonder where I was, to ever question whether I thought something else was more important than him. I'd not been able to take a yoga class or get a massage since his birth without feeling guilty for leaving him.

"I'm sure you're right, that Cooper is fine, it's just that this – the two of us, you and me – it's happened so fast. What if--?

"I love ye, Grace," he said, interrupting me. His eyes were locked with mine, his voice deep and husky with desire. "I've loved ye since the first time I saw ye. Before ye knew of my existence, I loved ye."

I'd fallen for a similar line once before and wound up pregnant and alone. But that profession of love had been laced with beer and lust, without tenderness or respect. This was different. I felt the truthfulness of Eoghanan's words somewhere deep inside of me.

It was not the first time I'd felt such a conviction—Eoghanan said nothing he didn't mean. I wouldn't either.

"I won't tell you that part of me doesn't worry that I'm just too caught up in this, that it's foolish for me to say it, because it wouldn't be true. I am worried. I'm scared to death, Eoghanan. I'm scared because I know what you mean. That first time in the kitchen, I felt something, too, and that seems completely crazy to me." I was rambling but I couldn't stop, my breath coming so rapidly I was dizzy. "It's completely crazy. I mean, who does this? Feels this way so fast? It's nuts."

Both of my hands lay on his shoulders, and I found that I was shaking him a bit.

Eoghanan regarded me, his expression confused. "I only understood mayhap three words of that, lass. That was a good deal too many words when all I can think about is how much I want you with me, tonight and every night. Please say it again, lass, only with less words."

I laughed, leaning in to kiss him gently before moving my lips to his ear. "I only meant, I love you, too."

He groaned, a deep delighted sound, and in that instant, lifted me into his arms, his mouth crushing mine as he carried me to his bed. He put me down beside it, turning me so that I faced him, taking both of my hands in his, he said, "I consider myself to be an honorable man, Grace. But the truth of the matter is, I doona wish to wait for a proper wedding before we come together as man and wife. I will, though, lass, if that is what ye want. Otherwise, the proper wedding can wait, and I will say my vows now before ye only, and God.

Tears of joy and love filled my eyes. How I adored his romantic heart. "Oh, Eoghanan," I said in a breathless whisper. "What wedding could be any more proper than that?"

I knew this impromptu "marriage" was only so that we could be together without Eoghanan feeling he'd "dishonored" me, and that it wasn't official. It really meant nothing binding, and I would not hold Eoghanan to it come morning. He was the one that needed it in order for us to make love, not me. I had no illusions; that is what this was about, and I was okay with it. Eoghanan was a man of his time, and I was a woman of mine. But we were in his world now, and I would go along with it for his sake.

He smiled. "I wish to have ye as my one and only, Grace, now and forever, until the end of time. Will ye be mine?"

"Yes," I whispered. Then, with a laugh of pure happiness, said more loudly, "Yes!" I squeezed his hands. "I wish to have you as my one and only, Eoghanan, now and forever, until the end of time. Will you be mine?"

"Nothing would please me more, lass." He squeezed my hands in return.

I grinned through my tear-glazed eyes. "I will love you, honor you, support you, protect you, and take care of you in sickness and in health, as long as we both live," I said, wishing, suddenly, that this *was* the real thing. A binding wedding to the man I knew now that I loved with all of my heart.

"And I will love ye, honor ye, support ye, protect ye, and take care of ye in sickness and in health, as long as we both live," he repeated. His sparkling eyes continued to hold mine as he added, "And I will love Cooper as if he were my own. I will protect and support him. I will strive to show him how to be a good man, by my own example."

In that moment, though I had not thought it possible, my love for Eoghanan doubled as my tears slipped free. We stepped into each other's arms and kissed, and I pretended this was a real wedding, binding us together as man and wife. For in my heart, at least, it was.

***

*H*ours later, as we held one another, kissing and snuggling and laughing, Eoghanan told me again that I was beautiful. He must have told me so a dozen times already tonight.

"I'm not beautiful, but thank-you. Ever since my pregnancy,

these things . . . " I motioned toward my stomach, now covered beneath the blankets. "I've tried everything. They won't fade away."

Eoghanan scowled. "Do ye forget I have my own scars, Grace?"

"That's different. Your scar is sort of . . . I don't know." I nuzzled closer to him and said in a mock-sultry voice, "It makes you look even more rugged."

"Rugged, aye?" He chuckled. "Those *things* as ye call them — yer own scars — they're reminders of the wonderful lad that ye created, lass. Ye should be proud of them, for they make ye even more beautiful than ye already are."

The way he said things...how could I not believe him. I nuzzled my face into the side of his neck, then tilted my head up to nibble the lobe of his ear. "Have I told you that I love you, husband?"

"Aye, but I'm happy to hear it again and again, as often as ye want to say so."

"I love you," I breathed into his ear.

"And I love ye, as well." He kissed me slowly, a soul-searing, heart-stopping kiss that left me breathless. "And tonight I plan to show ye just how much."

Tonight and for the rest of our lives, I thought. I wanted forever with Eoghanan more than anything. After the Conalls went home, freeing up my room, and our fairy tale of a marriage was no longer necessary, I hoped beyond hope that Eoghanan wanted it, too.

M y eyes slowly drifted closed. I was happy and exhausted. Just as I'd begun to dream, Eoghanan wrapped his arms around me and pinched my ear.

"Oh no, ye doona get to sleep yet, lass. Do ye not remember what I told ye?"

I opened one eye, leaving the other closed. "What's that?"

"I said I was going to show ye just how much I love ye tonight. I am not done with ye yet." He chuckled.

He had to be kidding. Was he not as exhausted as me? "Let's at least take a cat nap." I scooted in to him, moving my head to his chest.

"Ye are mad if ye think I'll be able to sleep with ye lying next to me like this." He pulled his head back to look at me. "Grace, what is a 'cat nap'?"

I yawned, stretching into him. "It's an expression. It just means a short nap."

He shook his head, sat up. "A short nap would turn into a long sleep."

"Mmmhmm..." I allowed my eyes to drift closed once again. This time he didn't argue.

He lay down again, pulling me close to him.

"Thank you," I whispered, planting a kiss on the side of his cheek.

"For what?" He grinned into my lips.

"For not allowing me to talk myself out of this." Voices traveled down the hallway outside his door, and I spoke to him, my voice teasing. "See? Everybody is going to bed. It's time to sleep."

"Aye, our guests are being shown to their rooms." He paused, his eyebrows scrunching up in the middle.

"What are you thinking?"

"I'm counting. I doona think we have enough bedchambers."

I smiled, laughing into his chest. "You didn't, but you do now."

"Did ye build us one, Grace? 'Tis a talent I dinna know ye had."

"No. Your mother kicked me out of my room."

"She what?" The covers flew back and he tried to leave the

bed, but I jumped up to stop him, grabbing his shoulders and pulling him backward.

"Cool your jets. She assigned me to another room."

"Aye? And whose room is that? I doona think Baodan will make room for ye in his bed." He grinned.

I rolled my eyes. "No. Your mother asked—instructed—me to sleep in your room."

"No, she dinna?" Eoghanan's eyes widened in disbelief.

"Yes. I promise you she did. I was rather surprised myself."

"Aye, I doona know what to say. I doona think I've ever been so surprised." He laughed a moment before reaching over and pulling me close again, drawing my head down to meet his kiss. "Ye wouldna want to disobey my mother, would ye?" he said.

CHAPTER 28

I slept until midday, only to find myself alone in Eoghanan's room when I woke. He meant it as a courtesy—rising before me so that we would not appear before the new guests at exactly the same time, coming from exactly the same direction. I'd been worried about it all night, so I relaxed upon finding myself alone.

"Mom!" Cooper shrieked from the hallway outside my door. "Hey, which room are you in, Mom?"

The little voice sent my heart pattering a million miles a minute, and I leapt from the bed in a panic looking for my dress so that I could slip it on before Cooper burst through the door. I managed it without a second to spare, reaching for the handle just as the door flung open.

"There you are, Mom! You missed breakfast by a long shot. Dad said you were around here somewhere." He peeked his head inside. "Isn't this E-o's room?"

I was suddenly very warm. "Umm...yeah, with all of the new people in the castle, I had to give up my room for the guests."

He shrugged. "Oh, okay, cool."

I smiled, kissing his temple as I walked out of the room with him still on my hip.

"Hey, guess what, Mom?"

"What, Coop?"

"There's even more people coming! Ba-o – that's my new name for Mitsy's husband – and another guy named Donal just told everyone. They said, like, a bunch of clans or something were coming. I don't know what a clan is, but it sounds like a lot of people are coming to stay here for a gathering."

He really emphasized the word *gathering*. It had clearly been spoken of as if it were something very special.

"Oh, yeah?"

"Yeah, I bet it's going to be tons of fun."

It was a reasonable thought for a child to have, and I imagined the men who had decided on such a gathering thought very much the same thing.

As for every woman in the castle, I could all but hear their internal groans, thinking that instead of tons of fun, it was going to be tons of work.

Cooper and I were greeted at the bottom of the stairs by Jeffrey. He smiled much too wide at the sight of me.

"Hey, Coop, I think Lady McMillan has a job for you if you're willing to help."

He immediately squirmed out of my arms. "Yeah, yeah, where is she?"

Jeffrey pointed in the direction of the kitchen. "That way, I believe."

"I bet I can find her. I think I'm gonna make a nickname for her too. Lady Mac, I think."

At the same time that Jeffrey shook his head, I said, "Uh, no, Coop. Sorry, but some people don't need nicknames."

"Oh, come on. I bet she'd like it."

I was sure he was right. Still, it was too casual a name.

"No. I agree with your mother," said Jeffrey. "You call her Lady McMillan. Understand?"

"Yes, sir." Cooper's face drooped for just a second, but he lifted it quickly, smiling and shrugging his shoulders before he took off toward the kitchen. "It was worth a shot, huh?" he said as he went, looking back at us over his shoulder.

Jeffrey and I laughed in unison as we watched him leave. As soon as he was out of earshot, Jeffrey turned to me, that same creepy grin on his face. "Good on you, Gracie."

I held up both hands in question. "What's with this 'good on you' stuff? Are you British or something? I'm pretty sure that's, like, a UK thing. And don't call me Gracie."

He laughed. "Hmm...I don't know, maybe it is. I've watched a lot of BBC in my day. Still, you get my drift." He nudged me gently with an elbow. "No need for you to try to look so innocent with me."

"I don't know what you're talking about."

His expression sobered, but the sparkle remained in his eyes. "I couldn't be happier for you, Grace. For both of you. I mean that."

I stepped forward and hugged him. "Thank you. I must admit, I'm happy for us, too. Eoghanan and I . . . it just feels *right*, you know?"

"No, I don't. Not personally, but I can imagine."

I stepped back, looked up at him. "So where is everybody? I guess it's time I show myself."

"They're all outside. You'll like them. Cool bunch. So...after last night...I guess that means we're staying?"

We started walking toward the outside doors together, and I turned my head to regard him skeptically. "I thought you were staying regardless?"

He smiled. "Forgive me, I am. I just misspoke. I meant to say, 'I guess that means you're staying?'"

"Yes, I'm staying."

"Good."

Just as we reached them, the grand doors of the castle swung open. Immediately, Mitsy latched onto me, sweeping me into the crowd.

"There you are, Grace." She held onto my arm but extended her neck to call after a group of women standing near the pond. "Bri, Blaire, Adelle, come meet Grace!" Three women, two of which I could have sworn were twins, all smiling, made their way to me. She pointed to the first woman bouncing a baby on her hip. "This is Bri." Shifting to the second woman, she said, "This is Blaire. I know they look like sisters, but they're not; although, most people think they are. Long story, Eoghanan can tell you sometime. And this," she smiled at the last woman, who was older than the others, "is Adelle, Bri's mother."

I smiled, shaking all of their hands. "Nice to meet you."

Mitsy allowed them no chance to respond, quickly yanking me toward another group of people, and so the routine continued until I had been introduced to everyone in their party.

"You're glad to have some people about, aren't you?"

Mitsy laughed, releasing her grip on me for the first time. "Yes. Sorry. The Conalls...we're all family. And Bri and I have been best friends a long time. I'm just happy for all of us to be in the same place. Plus...I'm glad to have some extra hands to help with this sudden gathering."

"Understandably so. I'll be happy to help in any way that you need me to."

"Thank you. And now..." she pointed at Eoghanan. "I'll release you for a while."

Mitsy flittered away quickly, and I made my way over to Eoghanan who, much to my surprise, gathered me up in his arms and kissed me rather thoroughly.

"Well, good morning to you, too." I laced my fingers with his as he led me away from the crowd and back inside the castle.

"Aye, 'tis a wonderful morning. Though, I'm afraid I have some unfortunate news."

Dread settled immediately in my gut. "What?"

He twirled a strand of my hair. "Doona look so worried, lass. 'Tis nothing all that bad. I'll be away tomorrow—down to the village to fetch supplies for the gathering. I expect the lassies will need yer help here."

"Oh, I don't mind helping. I already told Mitsy I'd do whatever they need me to."

"Aye, ye say that now, but ye doona yet know all the women who will be leading the charge around here tomorrow. Not only my mother, but also Rhona, our head maid and a lifelong resident of this castle. And if I know the Conalls, their Mary will be anxious to take charge of something. They'll need her help, I'm not saying that they won't, 'tis only that if Mary helps, then Adelle will jump in just to aggravate her."

"Sounds like you've been around them a lot."

He shook his head. "Not all that much, truthfully, but it doesna take verra long to see how a group of headstrong women behave when ye put them all to task on the same thing. 'Tis a powerful but frightening force."

CHAPTER 29

cMillan Territory Village

Eoghanan rode next to Eoin Conall, his cousin on his mother's side.

"I am pleased to see ye doing so well, cousin," Eoin said. "The blade wound was such that only one with Morna's powers could heal it."

Thinking back on that night, Eoghanan shuddered. Death had meant little to him then, but now he had much more to lose. The knowledge that death had been so close to him only a few months prior still made him uneasy. He couldn't imagine never having had the chance to know Grace or her bonny son.

"Aye, I am verra glad, as well. I owe the witch a great debt."

"I doubt Morna sees it that way."

Eoghanan nodded. "I know that she doesna, but it makes me feel no less indebted."

Cooper's voice from a short distance in front of him caught Eoghanan's attention. "Whoa, buddy!" the boy shouted.

"Whoa....Whoa...are you trying to make me fall off you? 'Cause you're doing a good job."

Giving his own horse a nudge, Eoghanan rode to catch up with him. When Cooper had insisted on having his own horse, they'd given him the oldest, gentlest beast in their stables. The horse was doing nothing to dismount Cooper, barely moving at a slow trot.

Still, Cooper had both arms wrapped around his horse's neck, his little chest pressed flat against the horse's mane.

"Have ye not ever ridden a horse before, Cooper?"

The child lifted his head just slightly, still maintaining his tight grip on the creature's neck.

"Of course, I haven't. I'm a city boy. Born and raised in NYC. The only horses I've ever seen were pulling those buggy things for tourists."

Eoghanan didn't know half of what the lad meant, but he believed that he'd not seen many horses. "Would ye like to ride with me, lad?"

"No. I gotta learn if I'm gonna live here, don't I?"

It pleased Eoghanan to no end that Cooper knew his parents planned to stay here. It made it seem more certain, more real. "Aye, ye will need to learn, but it doesna have to be today if ye doona wish it. I can teach ye back at the castle, when there are not so many others around."

Cooper shook his head, determined to keep going. "No, I don't care if they watch. It'll just take me a little time to get used to it."

"I admire yer stubbornness, Cooper. Look." He pointed to the village stretched out in the distance ahead. "We are almost there. I'll ride beside ye to the village edge where we will dismount and tie up our horses."

"Okay." Cooper lifted his chest, testing out his balance now that someone was there to help in the case of a fall. "If you insist."

ith disbelieving eyes, the young witch Jinty watched the group of men approaching the village. She remained shaded amongst the trees; although, if noticed, the men wouldn't know who she was or what role she'd played in the destruction of their family. Still, better not to be seen.

She wasn't interested in the Conalls; she knew them well enough—the tall dark-headed Scot and the blonde one, both as formidable as they'd always been, but utterly unimportant to her. The young boy she'd never seen before. There was only one that caught her attention, only one that sent rage rushing through her very fingertips, morphing into hatred as it settled inside her heart.

Eoghanan McMillan, who'd taken from her the one man who could have delivered her from a life of solitude. She'd thought the red-haired demon was dead. No one had seen him—the bastard McMillan brother—in many moons. Clearly death had reached for him—the scar running the length of his body showed her that much—but he'd survived. Perhaps death was too much a kindness for him. He deserved to be subjected to the same lonely life he'd forced her to live.

When her beloved, Niall McMillan, had come to her the first time, she'd been a young girl lost—left alone after the death of her grandmother, forced to survive with only her powers and the knowledge of herbs she'd inherited from her grandmother. He'd given her a purpose and his heart.

One task in exchange for a life spent together—to help him gain his place as laird. For years she'd worked for him, dutifully producing poisons, never asking questions, waiting for him to come to her, only accepting his love when he offered it.

They'd come so close to victory. Then Eoghanan had turned Baodan against Niall, and her beloved had met his death. No matter who ran the blade through him, Eoghanan was to blame.

Once again, she was alone in the world—the witch in the woods, shunned until one wished bad fortune to fall upon another.

Soon, that bad fortune would reach Eoghanan. She would make sure he was as lonely as she.

She watched the group of men closely, following a short distance behind them as they made their way through the village, stopping to gather men and supplies. There would be a gathering at the castle, and all were invited. It would be the perfect time to act against him, but first she needed to find his greatest weakness, the thing he loved most in the world, and rip it from him.

It would be a difficult job. The mysterious McMillan brother had no family of his own, no one had ever seen him in the company of a lass. But everyone cared about something. Jinty would find Eoghanan's weakness in time.

Infectious laughter drifted from the direction of the group, and Jinty's eye's rested on the child. Eoghanan had the boy in his arms, and the look in his eyes was unmistakable. He cared for him.

She couldn't imagine why or what role this young boy now played in Eoghanan's life, but there was no denying that he adored the child. Eoghanan watched over him with cautious eyes, stood near him at all times. Whatever the reason, today the child was in his charge.

There was still much she would have to learn, but the gathering would be the perfect place to do so. If the child was now a permanent fixture in Eoghanan's life, she could think of no greater revenge than to change that for him.

CHAPTER 30

As Eoghanan had predicted, there was plenty of chaos the next morning as the group of women—Mitsy, Kenna, Rhona, Mary, Adelle, Bri, Blaire, and myself—tried to direct everyone to specific tasks for the day. However, after a few hours of disagreements and power struggles, we all fell into a nice routine, each of us setting to our tasks with a dogged determination to have our jobs completed before the men returned.

I'd been paired with Mitsy for the day and found myself with the very easy and enjoyable task of overseeing Adelle's husband, Hew, Jeffrey, and a handful of other men as they set up tents for the other arriving guests.

"Are you sure I'm not needed anywhere else? I feel a bit guilty watching these guys work when all of the other women are busy inside."

Mitsy placed a hand on my arm to keep me from getting up. "I am absolutely sure. Believe me. Kenna, Rhona, Adelle, and Mary each have control over a quarter of the castle, which is just how they like it. They feel like they're playing boss, but they won't be in each other's way. Bri is busy with baby Ellie, and I'm too hot and pregnant to do much of anything. I don't want to be alone, so that's where you come in."

"Okay, but are you sure you don't want to hang with Bri and the baby? I could help with the work that way."

"No." She said the word quite urgently.

I realized that her impending motherhood had her scared to death. She didn't want to be around babies just yet. I understood completely. I'd been much the same way.

"Okay, I'll stay. It will all be all right, you know?" I relaxed, leaning back against the side of the castle, realizing that it was rather foolish to argue myself into more work. "It's scary, especially when you didn't grow up dreaming of being a mother." She looked surprised that I would infer this about her. "I didn't. But, I promise, you just take it one day at a time. This child will be the best thing that ever happens to you."

Her lip suddenly quivered, and I reached out to rub her shoulder, understanding all too well the swell of emotions pregnancy hormones could bring.

"I know that...it's just...gosh, I look at Bri, and she was born for this. I wasn't." Her chest started to shake as she struggled to hold back tears.

"Oh, Mitsy. That child..." I pointed to her belly, recreating the very words that Jeffery's father had said to me once during my pregnancy with Cooper. "You were handpicked to be its mother. There's no one else in the world that can raise that baby the way you were meant to. You're already a perfect match for one another, because that little soul was placed with you instead of someone else. Do you know how many millions of mothers it could have been sent to? But it was sent to you. So just love it and do your very best, and everything will be just as it should be."

She leaned against my shoulder, soaking my sleeve with tears. "Oh my God, Grace. That was sooo . . . " She paused to sniffle and sob. "That was so good." More sniffles. "Really. You should put that on a card or something. Thank you."

I patted her back gently as I looked at the camp that was slowly assembling behind the castle. Deciding it best to change the conversation to help pull Mitsy out of her sulk, I said, "So tell me a little bit about who will be here. It's all pretty hard to keep up with."

She laughed and nodded, wiping her eyes as she lifted herself off me. "Yes, it is. You don't need to worry about explaining your family's appearance here. Everyone will think we talk funny, but I've found if you just say that you grew up far away from here, people don't seem to question it too much. It's really with the Conalls and MacChristys that things get complicated—seeing as Bri and Blaire are uncanny look-alikes."

They truly were. "How so?"

"Well, Blaire is Donal MacChristy's real daughter. Until Bri's appearance, everyone thought he had just one. But they look so much alike that they couldn't very well say they weren't twins. No one would believe it."

It seemed a very tricky situation. "So how does one go about making everyone who's known the family their whole life believe that Donal had a secret daughter?"

"Good question. You don't. I mean, they've created a story, but anyone with half a brain questions it. Luckily, no one is apt to admit their doubts about Laird Conall, Laird MacChristy, or his brother, Lennox."

"There are two MacChristys?" Sheesh, I needed a notebook.

"Donal has a brother, you see. Here's how they now explain Bri: Donal's wife died giving birth to Blaire, but now he says that she gave birth to twins, and he was so worried about raising two daughters on his own that he sent one of them away to live with his brother, Lennox MacChristy."

"Of course."

She laughed, appreciating my sarcasm. "Yes. Naturally. Anyway, Lennox MacChristy is a perpetual nomad. He's moved his three sons all over the globe their entire lives, so it's not as if many people could prove that he'd not raised Donal's secret daughter."

"Ah." Slowly, it made more sense.

"Yes. Anyway, that's who is coming to the gathering. Donal's brother hasn't been in this part of Scotland in a long time. Since Donal and all of the Conalls are already here, it seemed the perfect time for one huge family reunion."

"Okay. Anybody else I should know about?"

"The Camerons will be coming, as well."

"The Camerons?"

Mitsy nodded, pointing into the woods. "Yes. Pretty small group, but still, they'll be here. Kenna's sister, Nairne," a shadow of the still new wound crossed Mitsy's face, but she masked it well, "she's dead now and so is her son, both by Niall's hand. Her widowed daughter-in-law, Wynda, still resides at Cameron Castle. She will be here with her children."

I couldn't imagine such loss or such evil. Niall had torn so many lives apart, lives that were still struggling to heal.

Mitsy must have been able to read my thoughts, for she echoed just exactly what I'd been thinking. "He was evil. He got what he deserved."

Eoghanan's scar flashed before my eyes, a permanent reminder of all the destruction Niall had caused. "I'm glad he's dead, too," I said quietly.

CHAPTER 31

*E*oghanan's arms came around me and I leaned into him, taking his hands in mine as I pointed toward Jeffrey. "Look at him."

The gathering was now in full swing. The castle had been turned into a constant bustle of activity. The grand dining hall was filled with people visiting, laughing, dancing, and in Jeffrey's case, flirting rather obviously.

"Aye, I see him. What about it?"

I couldn't pull my eyes away from Jeffrey and the widow Wynda Cameron. The way he fawned over her, smiling and lingering, it was like watching a zoo animal. "I've never seen him like that. He really likes her."

"Wynda?" Eoghanan's voice echoed surprise.

"Yes. Wynda. Someone just offered him food, and he dismissed it. I think he's quite taken with your cousin, Eoghanan."

He nipped playfully at my ear. "Aye, well I doona think she's taken a liking to him. She looks verra...distressed."

I nodded, my sympathy for Jeffrey building. For all his proclamations that he was an expert in such areas, he was as out of practice as I was. "Yes, I can see that, too. Should we save him from embarrassment?"

"No, I doona think so. I've need of one of yer kisses, at the moment." I pecked his cheek, and he narrowed his eyes at me and smiled in a way that made my pulse stutter, adding, "A kiss more substantial than that, lass. The sort that requires privacy, so that we don't make the other lads here envious of me."

I laughed. "You're crazy, you know that?" Winking, he nodded toward the doorway and said, "Come with me."

"Wait. Where's Cooper? Jeffrey's clearly distracted." I had a hard time pulling my eyes away from the train wreck.

"Last I saw the wee lad, he was torturing Lady Blaire. He'll keep himself occupied, Grace. I havena seen ye in days. I only wish to steal ye away for a few moments."

I faced him, wrapped my arms around him. "You've seen me every day. I've been sleeping right next to you."

"Aye, but I'm not seeing ye when I'm asleep. Readying for visitors has exhausted us all far too much. I am not so tired this night."

I was eager to spend some time alone with him, as well. Though I'd gone years without male companionship, it was as if once awakened to it, I couldn't go long without him before I started to feel a bit empty. I lowered my arms from around his neck and took his hand. "Let's go."

We had only taken a few steps when we met up with Lennox MacChristy and his three sons.

"Eoghanan, what a fine man ye've turned into," said Lennox. "Do ye remember me, son?"

Eoghanan placed a friendly hand on the man's shoulder. "Aye, o'course I do. It has been a long time."

The old man laughed, and his round stomach continued to shake after he stopped. "Aye, I think ye were no older than seven the last time I passed through these parts, and my sons werena with me then. Let me introduce ye."

"I'm sorry." Eoghanan held up a hand to stop him.

I glanced up at him, confused. It was very unlike him to be so abruptly rude.

"Please accept my apology; I'm afraid 'twill have to wait. There is something I must attend to right away."

He nodded at the group of men and quickly pulled me away, dragging me across the room toward a small alcove draped in darkness.

"Eoghanan, what's the matter with you? I think you could've waited the five minutes it would have taken to introduce yourself."

He nodded in the direction we were headed. "No, 'tis Cooper."

It was then that I noticed him standing with his back pressed against the side of the archway, looking up at the tall young woman standing in front of him. At first glance, nothing appeared menacing about the situation. He chatted with the woman just as comfortably as he did everyone else. It was Eoghanan's urgency that unnerved me.

"Do you know her?"

"No. I havena met her. I know all who should be here, and she is not among them."

He approached them, and I didn't miss the look of alarm in the woman's eyes as he did so. Eoghanan might not have known her, but she knew him well enough.

"Is this yer son? We were just discussing our shared love of partridge."

I looked at Cooper who locked eyes with me and subtly shook his head. I immediately stepped forward to grab his hand, answering before Eoghanan got the chance. "No, he's my son. I'm Grace." I extended my hand. "You are?"

"Just a traveler. My name is not important."

"Aye, lass. I'm afraid 'tis. Do ye not live in the village?"

Eoghanan took one step toward her, placing himself between Cooper and me.

"Mom," Cooper whispered to me quietly. "I don't even know what partridge is. Is it like a bird? I never said I liked a partridge."

I squeezed his hand and nodded. "I know."

Taking in our exchange, the woman realized she'd been caught in a lie and slowly backed away. "No, I doona live in the village. I was only passing by and noticed the gathering."

Eoghanan held his arm out and moved with her toward the outside doors. "Then, I think it best ye be on yer way. Safe travels."

Cooper and I waited as Eoghanan showed the woman outside. I bent to pick Cooper up, trying to get a read for how he felt.

"What did she say to you, Coop?"

"Umm..." He lifted his shoulders in a shrug. Clearly the encounter had freaked me out much more than it had him. "She just asked me if E-o was my dad or something. When I said no, she asked me who was and then you guys walked up."

He squirmed in my grasp. No matter how much I didn't want to admit it, he wasn't going to allow me to keep picking him up very much longer.

"Can you put me down, Mom? I don't want people to see you carrying me around. Besides, I gotta go find Dad."

"Why? What are you and Dad doing?"

"He said for the next dance he'd carry me on his shoulders."

I lowered him to the ground, and he danced off in his father's direction as Eoghanan walked back to me.

"What do you think that was all about?" I asked him.

"I doona know for sure, but I believe 'twas the witch Niall went to for his poisons; a witch who is verra soon to be dead."

CHAPTER 32

"I'm sorry. Say that again. The witch who gave Niall the poisons that killed Osla, incapacitated you, and made your mother ill is still alive?" It seemed unlikely that even with Eoghanan gone, that Baodan wouldn't have gone after the woman with a vengeance.

"Aye, Baodan had her cottage raided soon after they sent me forward, but she was gone and no one has seen her since. I hoped Niall had killed her before the end. He would have, had he succeeded."

I ran my hands up and down my arms to rub away the cold that had crept over my limbs. "Why would she come back here?" It didn't make sense. It seemed to me that an accomplice to murder would flee and never come back.

"I doona know. It worries me. I have not laid eyes on the lass until tonight, and I dinna like to see her with Cooper."

"No." I shook my head as Eoghanan pulled me in close to him. "I didn't, either. Cooper said she wanted to know if you were his father. Why would she ask that?"

His chin rested on the top of my head, and he twisted in gently. "I doona know. When the gathering is over, we will find her again. We canna do it now, for there are many here from the villages who have used her services before. She may have unlikely friends."

The search of the grounds took longer than he'd hoped, but it was worth it to ensure that everyone was safe. Eoghanan expected Cooper and Jeffrey were already sleeping, but he couldn't bring himself to wait another night to speak with them both.

He heard Cooper's voice on the first knock and breathed easier knowing he wouldn't be responsible for waking the child, especially when the lad slept so little to begin with.

"You want me to get it, Dad?"

Jeffrey's voice neared the doorway. "No, Coop. I got it. You just stay where you're at."

Eoghanan stepped back as the door opened. "I'm sorry to disrupt ye. Might I speak a moment with ye both?"

Jeffrey motioned for him to enter and Eoghanan moved inside where he was immediately forced to open his arms to catch the young child flying toward him as he jumped off the bed.

"Cooper, do ye not think 'tis past yer bedtime?"

"Well, usually, but tonight was a special night."

"Aye, 'twas indeed. I'm glad I've found ye awake. I need to speak with ye and yer da."

"Is something wrong?" Jeffrey asked. "Is Grace okay?"

It was Cooper who answered Jeffrey. "Everything's fine, Dad. Look at his face. If something was wrong, he'd look worried. He just looks kinda nervous."

Jeffrey moved to stand in front of Eoghanan and Cooper, reaching out to mess with his son's hair. "You are too perceptive, kiddo." Jeffrey looked away from his son, turning his attention to Eoghanan. "Why are you nervous?"

"'Cause he likes Mom." Cooper shook his head dramatically, speaking before Eoghanan had the chance. "And I mean *really* likes her. Isn't that right, E-o?"

Eoghanan deposited Cooper back onto the bed. Facing both the boy and Jeffrey, he said, "Aye, 'tis yer mother I wish to speak to ye both about."

"Okay. Let's hear it." Jeffrey crossed his arms waiting for Eoghanan's explanation. Cooper glanced over at his father and mimicked him, crossing his own arms right alongside him.

Taking a breath for courage, Eoghanan said, "I know that the three of ye are a family, and I want ye to know that I doona ever wish to disrupt it, but 'tis my hope that ye are open to adding another member. I am verra much in love with Grace. I canna imagine my life without her." He locked eyes with Cooper. "Or without ye, Cooper. 'Tis my intention to ask Grace to marry me officially, but I willna do so without having both yer blessings. Do I have them?"

Cooper smiled back at him. "Whoa. That's a big question, E-o."

Jeffrey continued to regard him pensively, his arms crossed, guarded. "So, what do you mean by 'officially?'"

"I am already married to her in my heart, and will remain so. And she to me. But I will let her go if I must, while still remaining so."

Jeffrey's mouth quivered, as if holding back a smile. "So are you saying that if either of us said no, you really wouldn't ask her to 'officially' marry you? That's a big statement, my man."

Eoghanan nodded. He wouldn't. Committing to Grace in a way that all the world would know meant committing to her family, and he wanted both of them to accept him willingly. "Aye, I wouldna. I give ye my word."

"But Dad..." Cooper reached out to tug on his dad's arm. "You already told me we were gonna stay, so we're gonna tell him yes, right?"

Eoghanan did his best not to smile, wishing to allow Jeffrey the chance to answer.

Jeffrey turned to speak below his breath to Cooper but did it so that Eoghanan could hear him. "Well, of course we're going to tell him yes, but I was just trying to make him sweat a little."

"That's not very nice, Dad." Cooper lifted one eyebrow as he stared at his father – a gesture of disapproval.

"You're right. It's not nice. I apologize." Jeffrey turned back toward Eoghanan. "Yes, you have our full permission to ask her to marry you. I think you're a good man, Eoghanan. Do not prove me wrong."

Eoghanan extended his hand to shake with Jeffrey. "I swear to ye that I will do everything in my power to make her happy."

Jeffrey took his hand, shaking it just a little too firmly. "I'm serious, okay? I don't care if you're eight inches taller than me and the size of a professional football player. You hurt Grace, and I will hurt you. Understood?"

"Aye, I do. It pleases me that Grace has so many who care for her." Eoghanan stepped toward Cooper, shaking his little hand, too, to seal their agreement. "I will bid ye goodnight now. I thank ye both."

Eoghanan shut the door behind him, but not before he heard Cooper laughing at his father.

"You're a funny guy, Dad. You wouldn't even step on that spider earlier. I mean, come on, what do you think you're gonna do to E-o?"

CHAPTER 33

It took me the rest of the evening to wrangle my stress over the incident to a manageable size. I couldn't stand the thought of someone so evil standing so close to my son. Eoghanan had left immediately to find Baodan, and together they went with a small group of men to ensure the witch hadn't remained anywhere on the property.

When I saw Jeffrey leave the dining hall with Cooper in tow, I decided to take my leave, as well, stopping to ensure they made it safely to their bedchamber before making my way up to Eoghanan's room.

Once inside, I didn't bother to disrobe before collapsing onto the center of the large bed, the stress of the evening making me weak-limbed and exhausted. I wouldn't sleep, not until the men were back and I knew that the grounds were safe. Still, I tried to unwind a bit by rubbing my eyelids with my thumb and middle finger.

The repetitive motion must have done the trick, for I didn't hear Eoghanan enter until he spoke.

"Are ye trying to poke yer eye out, lass?"

The unexpected sound of his voice made me jump, and I sat up as he neared me, blinking oddly.

"No, but I think I just about managed it just now. You scared me."

"I'm sorry. I meant to be quiet so that if ye were sleeping, I wouldna wake ye."

I stood and moved to him, reaching up to kiss him warmly. "Did you find anything?"

He shook his head, pulling me closer.

"No, I doona think she will be back. Ye needn't worry yerself over it."

I didn't think for a moment that he really believed what he said. He was too smart not to realize that she wouldn't have taken such a risk to come here unless it was for a reason. Still, there was nothing to be done about it tonight, and I wanted to try to put the incident out of my mind. That wouldn't be easy to do.

"Hold me," I said to Eoghanan, my voice shaky and breathless, afraid. I needed the comforting refuge of his body.

He lifted my chin from its resting place against his chest. "I would love nothing more than to hold ye, Grace, but I want ye to know first that I will let no one hurt Cooper. Now or ever. Do ye trust me?"

His eyes were serious, fearless, confident. My anxiety melted away. "I trust you more than I've ever trusted anyone."

He gathered me into his arms then, his strength and warmth enveloping me like a shield. "I will hold ye now for as long as ye need."

I hugged him tightly. "I already feel better," I said. "Let's sit down and talk."

"Talk?" Leaning away from me, he smirked a little, his brows drawing together. "I liked the idea of holding ye better."

"I twisted out of his embrace and sat down on the edge of the bed. "Be serious, would you? It hit me today that there are still so many things we don't know about each other. I thought we could ask each other questions."

"Questions?" He frowned. "Do ye mean like the lawyers from yer time do in a trial? I saw it once on a television show when I was confined to my bed and healing at Morna and Jerry's inn. It dinna look like the participants were having any fun."

Eoghanan sat beside me. "No, not like that. I don't want to interrogate you or you me, like we're some kind of criminals. I want to know about you—your likes and dislikes, your hopes and fears, your life. And I want you to find out about mine."

I leaned back against the pillows and he did the same. "Can we ask one another anything?" he said.

"Yes, anything. Of course. Why don't we each ask three questions? If we want more after, we can go from there."

"I doona need many questions, lass. I already know what I wish to ask ye."

"Is that so? Ok, shoot."

"Shoot?" His brows pulled together in confusion.

"It just means 'start.'"

"Oh, aye, fine. My first question is, do ye miss yer own time?"

"No." My answer slipped out even more easily than I'd expected, but it was true. "There are exactly three things I miss about the twenty-first century." I hesitated. "Okay, maybe more than three, but only three that seem very significant to me. Number one, refrigerator ice; number two, toothpaste; number three, Bebop."

He nodded. "I understand. Having never met Bebop, I doona miss him, but I do myself miss refrigerator ice and toothpaste. We should have Morna send us some, aye, lass?"

"Toothpaste, yes. The ice would likely melt on the way, don't you think?"

"Aye, ye are right." He narrowed his eyes, as if thinking, then said, "Now for my second question. I couldna love Cooper any more if he was my own, but do ye wish for more children, Grace?"

A flush of warmth rose up to my face and my heart beat in overtime at the happiness that filled it at Eoghanan's confession that he loved my son. I loved how he loved Cooper. "Yes, I want more children. Many more."

He smiled, and I knew that my answer pleased him. I could see the future children I'd always dreamed of, all with the same red hair, same full lips as Eoghanan. I wanted those children to be his. I wanted to *really* marry him, and I hoped he felt the same and would make it happen one day. I realized that it was too soon to want such a thing. We hadn't known each other long; I needed to be patient and give him time to be sure. But it wasn't easy.

"My third question is this—do ye trust me to care for ye and Cooper? To love ye and protect ye and be there for ye always as I promised to do when we made our vows to each other on our first night together as man and wife in this room?"

"Our pretend vows, you mean?" I asked, my voice barely louder than a whisper.

A shadow darkened Eoghanan's eyes, and his face fell. "I dinna think we were pretending, Grace. I meant every promise I made to ye that night. Were ye only pretending when ye made the same promises to me?"

I shook my head. "No, but . . . It wasn't a formal ceremony—a legal, binding one. I understand you were just eager for us to be together. I can't expect to hold you to any promise of forever based on –"

"Ye verra well should expect it," he interrupted, his voice low and firm. "When I make a vow, I keep it, Grace. I doona take it lightly, formal or not. Legal or not." He paused, held my gaze. "But ye deserve both formal and legal, and so I will ask ye again . . . . Do ye trust me to care for ye and Cooper? To love ye and protect ye and be there for ye always"

My breath caught. It was more than one question, but I said nothing about it, my head getting a bit light as he took hold of my hand and stared at me with pleading eyes.

I exhaled. "Yes, Eoghanan, I trust you completely to do all that you said."

"And I, ye, lass." Relief flooded his eyes and he smiled. Standing, and drawing me to my feet, as well, he faced me, took both of my hands in his, and again held my gaze. "I know ye said only three questions, but I have one more: Will ye marry me, Grace, legally, as ye say, in a formal ceremony where we can bind ourselves to one another and profess our love in front of all who care for us most?"

CHAPTER 34

*E*oghanan's proposal was sweet and perfect, and my vision was blurred by tears as I answered him.

"Yes." I stepped forward to kiss him, my fingers stroking his face, my heart in his hands. "I would love nothing more, but I think there's someone else you might need to speak to before we make it completely official."

He brushed a tear away from my cheek and nodded while he smiled down at me. "Aye, two others that I counted. I've already spoken to both Cooper and Jeffrey."

"No. You haven't, have you?" I kissed him again. He was always thoughtful; it shouldn't continually surprise me, but every time it did.

"Aye, and they have both given their blessing. Though, if I hurt ye, Jeffrey has promised to cause me great harm."

I laughed. "I'm sure he had you shaking in your boots, huh?"

His eyebrows pinched together in the adorable way they always did when he didn't understand one of my modern expressions.

"Never mind," I said. "I love you."

"And I love ye, lass. Ye will never truly know just how much."

I stepped back, sat on the bed again. "I don't mean to spoil the moment, but I think it's my turn to ask questions now." I fanned my face. "Then I need to get out of this dress. It's getting stuffy in here."

One side of his mouth quirked up. He looked at me expectantly and sat down beside me again. Watching me closely, he said, "Please lass, 'tis now yer turn. Ask me whatever ye wish."

Compared to his questions, mine seemed like fluff, but to me they weren't. I could tell a lot about a person by the small stuff.

"Okay," I said, shaking myself out, allowing a breeze to work its way under the fabric of my clothing. "First question. Do you like dogs?"

I'd never had one myself, although I'd always wanted one. I didn't trust anyone that said 'no' to that question.

"Aye, there are few animals that I doona like."

"Good answer." I untied my shoes and kicked them off, sending them sailing across the room. "Second question. When you're holding a child and they decide to use your sleeve..." I paused, thinking on his normal attire, "okay, let's pretend that you're usually wearing a shirt. Anyhow, a child decides to use your sleeve as a nose tissue, are you quick to anger and show disgust?"

He laughed loudly, emphasizing the tight muscles in his stomach. "Why would I get angry, lass, when I use my shirt for just the same purpose?"

I let loose one uncomfortable chuckle, praying that he joked. "Question number three. What was your father like?"

In my opinion, this was perhaps the most important question. Men often turned into their dads, just like women did their mothers. If my parents had birthed boys, I had no doubt they would have turned into mini-me, terrifying versions of my father, just as Jeffrey had become the most admirable of men, like his own dad.

"Ah. I doona believe we have spoken of this before. The father that raised me was a kind, honest, decent man, but he was not my father by birth."

"Oh." Another reason, perhaps, that Eoghanan had taken so graciously to my strange relationship with Jeffrey. He, too, had grown up with another man standing in the stead of his real father. "So, did you know your real father?"

He clucked his tongue at me and scowled in a teasing way. "That makes four questions, does it not?."

I smirked back at him. "As I recall, you asked a fourth question, too. Now, answer mine."

He exhaled slowly. "No, I doona know who my real father was. My mother worked for the McMillans. When she became pregnant, they protected her. After she died giving birth to me, they took me in and raised me as their son."

I pointed to his red, curly mane, which was already starting to grow rather unruly, despite my recent cut. "I should have realized, with the red hair and all. You look nothing like Baodan." He nodded, but said nothing so I continued. "I request three more questions."

"Request granted, lass, but they will come at a cost." Looking completely serious, he added, "Three kisses in exchange."

I grinned and complied with his demand, brushing my lips against his, again and again and again, lingering.

"And, in addition," he murmured against my mouth, "we must remove these clothes we wore to the gathering, as I am also too warm and uncomfortable."

"Agreed," I said, and we both stood and stripped down to our undergarments. Scooting onto the bed, we propped up on the pillows next to one another, and I snuggled up to him, pulling the top sheet over us.

Eoghanan groaned with pleasure. "Aye, that is much better. Now . . . your questions, lass?"

"Okay. Would you rather be hot, or cold?"

"Cold."

Fair enough. With a laugh, I whipped the sheet off of him.

"Why did ye do that, lass?" Eoghanan asked, looking baffled.

"You said you like to be cold."

"Ye only gave me two choices: hot or cold. Warm is my preference." He tugged the sheet up again and we resumed our position of snuggling.

"I was only playing with you," I said, nibbling his ear. "Next question."

"Should I be afraid, lass?" He nuzzled my neck.

"Maybe," I teased. "But there's no getting out of this. What's your biggest pet peeve?"

His brows pinched in again. "I doona know what a 'peeve' is, lass."

"What's the one thing that drives you crazy? That you can't stand?"

"Ah. The sound of rain."

My hands flew up in surprise and my voice came out all high and pitchy. "What? Who doesn't like the sound of rain?"

"Me, lass. The sound of rain makes me think of water, and I doona like to swim. That, and it always makes me need to relieve myself something dreadful."

I laughed. "That is so weird. Sorry, but that's one strike."

"What do ye mean by strike?"

I was really going to have to cool it with the modern references. "It's a sports thing. If you get three strikes, you're out."

He shifted out of my arms suddenly and sat up. "Out, lass? Are ye giving me some sort of test? Ye do know that ye've already agreed to marry me, aye?"

"Yeah, but two more strikes, and I'm gonna have to back out."

A flash of panic crossed his face. "'Tis not an option, Grace."

I winked at him. "You really are going to have to learn when I'm teasing you, Eoghanan."

He exhaled noisily and stretched out beside me again. "Ye are a cruel woman, lass."

Chuckling, I said, "Okay, I think this is my last question, actually. Then maybe we can get some sleep. That sound okay?"

His warm hands caressed my back. "Aye." He yawned. "But there will be more kisses first in exchange for yer last question. Before the sleeping, I mean."

"Hmmm. I think I can handle that. In fact, I'm sure I can." I yawned, too, then almost purred with pleasure at the feel of his hands massaging my back. "Okay, what do you think the word 'girlfriend' means?"

"'Tis a strange question, lass. Doona ye think the name itself tells its meaning. It refers to lassies who are my friends."

I shifted away from him slightly so I could see his face, and my finger went up like a stern school teacher. "Wrong. I know that's not a word used here, so it's okay, but let's just clear that up right now. Your girlfriend is what I was to you right before I became your fiancé. The first time you used that word in front of me, I thought you were gleefully admitting to being with your brother's wife."

His sleepy, half-closed eyes, suddenly opened to the size of saucers. "Ach, I dinna ever mean that."

"Yeah, I know. Now come here. I'm ready to pay up."

Regarding me quizzically, he said, "Pay up?"

"You said that last question would cost me more kisses."

"Oh, aye, I did, didn't I?" Grinning, he scooted closer to me, and I tilted my face up to his neck, trailing my lips up to his ear so that I could whisper into it.

"I have one last question. Where would you like me to start?"

CHAPTER 35

*S*leepless nights filled with loving Eoghanan differed greatly from sleepless nights in the office working on magazine articles or sleepless nights tending to a sick child. When the sun rose the next morning and my eyes had yet to close for a single minute, I realized that while my body was beyond exhausted, my mind was alert and happy.

"What's the plan for the day?" I rolled to face him, Eoghanan's deep green eyes piercing into my soul.

He said nothing for a moment, and I could sense that he hesitated. "Not verra much. If ye doona mind, I'd like to make the announcement of our coming marriage today."

I didn't mind at all. If Vegas had been only an airplane flight away rather than several hundreds of years, I would have suggested we marry the very next day. I moved to run my hands through his hair, kissing his nose as I snuggled into him. "I don't mind at all. How soon can we be married? I mean, I'm not very familiar with how weddings work here."

He rolled over onto his stomach, propping himself up on his elbows as he looked down at me. "As soon as ye wish, lass. I dinna wish to rush if ye wanted to take some time, but I'd marry ye today if I could."

"Today? Could things be arranged so quickly?" I closed my eyes and smiled, delighting in the feeling of his fingertips as he ran feather-light touches up and down my bare arm.

"'Tis not so much to arrange, but I'm afraid I must leave for a day or two to make special preparations."

"Preparations for what?" Fear that I'd managed to lock away for the night escaped and returned to taunt me. "You're not... Eoghanan, I don't want you to go after that witch."

"No, lass. I am not afraid of Jinty. Without my brother to act as her puppet master, I doona think she is capable of real harm. Though should I get the chance to end her life, I will do so for all the pain she helped bring upon this family. 'Tis only that I wish to prepare a surprise for ye. Baodan and I will leave this afternoon."

I knew it was ridiculous to feel sad about that. I was a grown woman, and shouldn't allow such a notion to find a resting place in my mind, but the thought of him being away for a mere two days unsettled me. "Must you leave? In the middle of the gathering?"

"Doona worry yerself, Grace. The gathering will last for weeks. Few will even notice our departure. Eoin and Arran will be here to care for things in our absence. Trust me, when ye see what I've planned for ye, ye will be glad I left." He flipped over onto his back and stood rather abruptly. "In the meantime, I need ye to stay here a moment while I check on yer other surprise."

He dressed quickly and left, leaving me with a mind full of confused wonderings. He'd not left my side all night. How could he have so many plans already in place?

He didn't leave me long to imagine what he had planned, arriving back in the doorway within a matter of minutes, the largest smile I'd ever seen on his face.

"I think ye best get dressed, Grace."

I stood and did as he asked. His excitement roused my curiosity greatly. "Okay, what is it? What have you done?"

He shrugged nonchalantly. "'Tis not so much what I have done, but Morna. Ye see, I had a conversation with wee Cooper before we traveled back here, and he spoke of a man verra important to ye all. When I told Morna of him, she promised that she would check in often to see how things progressed between us, and should they lead to marriage, she would send ye, Cooper, and Jeffrey a gift. Yer gift has arrived."

Surely he couldn't mean Bebop! The man the three of us leaned on more than any other and the last missing piece in our little puzzle couldn't possibly be here.

I fumbled with the laces on my clothing in my anticipation and eventually spun my back toward Eoghanan, lifting my hair and pointing to my back. "Help me, please."

He obliged, working quickly. "There. Ye are properly covered and free to go and see yer surprise. I hope ye are not disappointed."

I hoped so, too. He'd built up to it so much, making me believe it could only be one thing, that I knew if it wasn't, I would have a difficult time masking my disappointment.

I walked quickly down the hallway, unsure of just where my surprise waited. Then I heard it—the same voice that I'd gone to my entire life for guidance and comfort, the same voice that Cooper loved second only to mine and Jeffrey's.

I turned the corner and nearly wept. There, with Cooper clinging to him, grasping his neck so tightly I was surprised he could breathe, stood Bebop.

<hr>

"So one day, I was sitting on my back deck fishing, and I closed my eyes for just a moment," Bebop winked at me, "resting my eyes as I do, and the next moment I'm sitting in a stranger's living room with an old man and woman staring back at me."

He had us all enraptured—Cooper, Jeffrey, Eoghanan, and me all standing around him, listening intently to his tale of how Morna had brought him here. He had the unique ability to tell any story, even everyday stories that weren't truly as interesting as the one he told now, as if they were the grandest of tales.

No wonder my son had such a vivid imagination and that he'd developed an early love of books. Who wouldn't with a grandfather like Bebop? He was the sort of man one could listen to for hours.

Bebop, whose real name was Charles Oakes, was a good decade older than both of my parents. He and Maggie had given birth to Jeffrey later in life, after over a decade of trying to have children. Bebop stood the same average height as Jeffrey, about five-seven, although his shoulders now hunched a little, making him look shorter than he really was. An avid cyclist, he was in phenomenal shape for a man his age, but he still looked very grandfatherly—like a surprisingly sprite Gepetto.

He still had a full head of hair, but it was entirely gray, and he wore a pair of spectacles that often lingered on the end of his nose. Laughing as he spoke, he continued relaying his tale.

"Well, I'll tell you. For a moment I thought my mind had either caught up with the age of my body, or I'd had a heart attack sitting right on my deck and heaven was just very different than I'd ever imagined it."

Still in Bebop's arms, Cooper leaned back and gripped either side of the man's face, as if he couldn't believe he was really here. "So how did she make you believe everything? These two," he pointed to me and his father, "had a real hard time with it."

Bebop leaned in and pressed his forehead to Cooper's, speaking only to him. "Did your mother read you the story that your dad and I picked out for you?"

Cooper nodded, their foreheads still touching. "Yeah, I loved it, Bebop. When I first saw E-o, I thought maybe he was like that little prince in the book, and he'd come here on a spaceship."

Bebop pulled back, his cheeks still framed by Cooper's little hands. "Well, I'm not ruined like the grown-ups in the book. I can still see things like a child. I've always believed in a bit of magic." He turned his head to the side to look at us "ruined" grown-ups. "But, I'll tell you . . . I don't know if I could have dreamed up something like this. How very exciting." He shifted Cooper into his left arm and reached up to grip his head with his right hand. "Now I just need someone around here to give me something to help with this bloody bad headache."

CHAPTER 36

"How's my sweet girl doing?" asked Bebop. "You look stunning."

I turned and threw my arms around him, still stunned and delighted at his sudden appearance here. "I'm great. How's your head?"

"Oh, that." He dismissed his headache with a wave of his hand. "Much better, actually. I have to tell you, Grace, the last time I saw you in a dress about to walk down the aisle, the sight made me ill."

I snorted, laughing into his shoulder. It had made me ill, as well. "Gee, thanks."

"You know what I mean, Grace. My heart was broken for you that you planned to do something so foolish as to marry my son. This is very different. I don't pretend to know the man you plan to marry, but it feels very right to me. And my gut is always worth trusting."

It was. Bebop's advice was something I'd never taken lightly.

"Thank you. I can't tell you how glad I am that you're here. It seems rather impossible to me."

"Less impossible to you than me, I imagine. Childlike I may

be, but truthfully, all of this is a lot to take in." He paused, releasing me so that I could glance one last time into the mirror. "Can I tell you a story?"

I would never turn down a Bebop story. "Of course you can."

"Good. Are you ready? I'll tell you while we walk down."

"Yes." I smiled and looped my arm through his.

I wasn't altogether sure where exactly the wedding would take place. We'd announced our impending nuptials the morning after Bebop arrived, but had decided to have a private ceremony with only the closest of family. Cooper, Jeffrey, and Bebop on my side. Baodan, Mitsy, and Kenna on Eoghanan's.

As a result, there'd been very little to prepare, and I gladly allowed Eoghanan to plan all of the little surprises he seemed so intent upon.

As we moved down the hallway from the bedchamber where I'd readied myself with the help of Mitsy and Kenna, Bebop began his story. "Do you remember what I told you when you were pregnant with Cooper? When you were so worried that you would be a terrible mother?"

I smiled, he had no way of knowing just how well I remembered every word of what he'd told me that day. "Of course I do."

"Maggie hated that story. It was what I used to tell myself every time she miscarried. For all those years that we tried to have a child, I would rationalize the loss by saying, 'That soul wasn't meant for us. Ours is coming.' I could always tell it made her angry. She felt that me saying that made it seem like children born to abusive, cruel parents were meant to be placed in such situations, and she couldn't stand it. Of course, that's not how I meant it. It just made me feel like I hadn't lost something; that the person meant for me was still on the way to us. And, of course, he was—Jeffrey."

By this point we were already nearing the main doorways of the castle, and it surprised me to find the hallways and other rooms entirely empty. Either there would be many more guests at our wedding than I anticipated, or they'd been instructed to clear out until after the wedding. I hoped it was the latter. Still, I could tell we neared our destination, for Bebop slowed his pace markedly, clearly not finished with his story.

"As I said, Maggie hated when I would say that, taking my words too literally when they were only meant to soothe my heart each time after a new loss. She never said anything about it though until after you entered our life."

I couldn't imagine what I had to do with it.

"We already had Jeffrey at that point, but to our surprise Maggie became pregnant again, only to miscarry the child a few weeks later. As per usual, I said something about the child not being meant for us and for the first time in a decade, she lost it on me. She said that I was a fool to think such a thing when we had the likes of you to show us what an untrue notion that was.

"She said that anyone with half a brain could see that your parents didn't come close to deserving you and that if you were meant to be anyone's child, it was ours." He paused and brought my hand up to his lips, kissing it gently. "I understood then how stupid it was, but it had brought me comfort when I needed it so I never spoke it again until I told it to you when you were pregnant because, really, Maggie was right."

I'd never looked at it as Maggie had either, but it was certainly a way of thinking that could be seen from several viewpoints. As a soon-to-be mother, I'd taken it as Mitsy had, words to calm my doubt that I could be the mother I wanted to be for my child. For someone more empathetic to the woes of others, as Maggie had been, or as a child who'd grown up under terrible circumstances, I could see how the thought could be seen as placing uncalled-for guilt on a blameless child. No child is meant to grow up in anything less than a loving and caring home.

Still, I didn't understand what Bebop telling me all of this had to do with my getting married in a matter of moments. "Okay, forgive me, Charles. What are you trying to say?"

"Only this, Grace." He stopped walking.

I looked up to see that we were at the end of the path leading to the secluded tree with the low hanging branch—Eoghanan's special place for thinking, where he'd taken me the night Cooper and Jeffrey had disappeared. It would be good to make a new, happier, less-stressed memory in this place.

"That is always how Maggie saw you...as hers, no matter who you were born to. While I know that your real parents aren't here to see you marry the man you're meant to, I am here, and," he choked up slightly and I squeezed his hands in comfort, "she is watching all of this from heaven and beaming. I couldn't love you or be any more proud of you than I am right now."

I was full out crying now, and Bebop moved quickly to dab the tears from my face, shaking his head in apology. "Forgive me; I'm a stupid man. I didn't mean to make you cry."

"No, you didn't." I leaned forward and kissed him on the cheek. "Thank you. My whole life, I wanted to be your child; to know that you wanted me as much as I did you. Nothing could be more pleasing to hear than what you just told me." Inhaling to regain my composure, I turned so that I faced the front of the tree-lined path that served as my aisle. "I love you, Charles. Now, let's get me married, shall we?"

* * *

I wondered just how many brides could recall very much about the actual ceremony part of their wedding, for as it drew to a close and Eoghanan leaned in to kiss me, I realized that I'd been rather lost in a haze of happiness, my emotions so swelled that I couldn't remember anything.

I felt his lips touch mine and guilt swarmed me, until he leaned in and whispered in my ear, "Ye have made me the happiest man in the world, lass. I am now officially yers forever, and ye are mine."

It didn't matter that I couldn't remember the ceremony, or just exactly what words had been said; I remembered the private vows we'd exchanged many nights ago, and besides, the last words he'd whispered to me just now were what a wedding was really about. They were all that truly mattered.

I just wished I could shake the feeling that everything was going a little *too* well.

CHAPTER 37

$\mathcal{E}$oghanan McMillan was an utter fool if he thought banning her from McMillan land would protect them. Jinty had other ways to keep herself abreast of what went on in the castle, other ways to look for the perfect opportunity to take the boy.

She'd been right to think the child was special to him. The warning in his eyes had been clear enough that day he'd seen her inside the castle. She'd known he suspected who she was, but that didn't matter in the least.

Jinty watched them now—Eoghanan and his new bride riding away from the castle. They would be gone for days, the boy left in the care of his real father, a man far less threatening than Eoghanan. She would continue to watch the child closely and, at the opportune time, she would take him away.

Eoghanan would return to find his new son gone.

"If ye look back in the direction of the castle once more, lass, I shall turn my horse around, and we will go home."

"I'm sorry." I turned my head around and leaned into him, kissing the underside of his chin. McMillan Castle was far from view by now, but for whatever reason, looking back toward the castle helped to ease my nervousness at leaving Cooper.

He'd be fine, of course. He stayed with his father at least two nights a week back in New York, but for some reason, I was irked by an unexplainable sense of worry. Whether it was the newness of our situation or the vastness of the castle and its endless opportunities for Cooper to get in trouble, I didn't know. But it wasn't fair of me to give Eoghanan anything less than my full attention.

"How much farther are you taking me?" I reached my arms up behind his head, gently massaging the back of his scalp while I leaned into him, just as I'd done the day I'd cut his hair.

He let loose a deep contented sigh of enjoyment. "Ach, Grace, I love the way that feels, with yer fingers in my hair."

Following our wedding, we had joined the others residing at the castle for the gathering at a large celebratory dinner that lasted well into the wee hours of the morning. We were both so completely exhausted when we collapsed into bed afterward that thoughts of binding our official marriage vows through consummation hadn't crossed our minds for a moment.

Interrupting my thoughts, Eoghanan said, "We have at least a full day more ahead of us."

"Might we stop for a while now?"

"Stop? Why? 'Twould only delay us further."

I laughed against him, rather shocked at his daftness. I reached behind him and pulled at the hair along the base of his neck. "I want my *husband*," I emphasized the word, drawing it out and speaking in the most seductive voice I could manage. It sounded rather ridiculous to me, but it seemed to do the trick for him just fine. "I want —"

He pulled the horse to a stop before I even finished, his breathing ragged in my ear.

Flinging himself off the side of the horse so that he could pull me off with him, he said, "Hush yer mouth, Grace, so I can kiss it." He hurriedly pulled me toward a secluded area amongst the trees, his chest rising and falling quickly with each step. He didn't look back at me until he stopped walking, spinning to back me up against a wide-based tree, his cheek leaning forward to press flush against mine. "'Tis verra shocking for a wife to ask her husband for such."

"Is it?" I enjoyed this exchange, so different from any we'd had before. True, as a woman, I loved being pursued, for him to make the move and let me know how much he desired me. Eoghanan certainly did those things. However, I was a woman of my own time, and sometimes I wished to be the one to pursue, to surprise, to show him the depth of my desire without him instigating it.

"Aye, 'tis shocking for proper women of this time, Grace. But I canna say I don't like hearing ye ask. 'Tis even more shocking for ye to want to love me outside, with nothing but the sky above us, nothing to hide us should someone pass by. Do ye mean it?" He drew me even closer.

I smiled against his cheek, then shifted to kiss him slowly, thoroughly, breathing in his scent of soap and wood smoke, fresh air and man. When we broke apart, I asked, "Do I seem like I'm teasing you? I care far too much about you to ask for something I don't really want from you. Besides . . . " I glanced around at the barren countryside; there wasn't another person in sight as far as the eye could see, no sounds to indicate that someone not yet visible might be approaching. There were only birds and trees, shimmering grass and buzzing insects. "It doesn't appear this road is widely traveled." Winking, I added, "Aye?" mimicking his accent playfully.

Abruptly, he left my side and quickly made his way to his horse, returning with a blanket he'd taken from the back of the animal. He wasted no time finding a spot on the ground beneath the shade of the tree where the grass was soft and the incline flat. He spread the blanket across it and we stretched out atop it, side-by-side, facing each other.

Then we forgot about time or how much farther we had to go before reaching our destination. We forgot about propriety and the birds looking down from the branches above us and the insects crawling on the blades of grass nearby. We made love to the sound of buzzing and chirping, and it became our song, one we'd never forget for the rest of our lives—a serenade to our first day as an *officially* married couple, although we'd already been married much longer in our hearts.

CHAPTER 38

Many miles away from the meadow where we'd stopped, Eoghanan dismounted our horse. "We canna ride the horse the rest of the way. I'll leave him with a man I know in the village. We must make the rest of the way on foot."

I nodded, flipping myself over so I could slide off the horse, as well. "Thank God." I was tired of being jostled around on the back of the beast and ready to have my feet on the ground again.

After one more day of riding, we had arrived at the smallest of villages that sat at the base of a tall cliff. Only one trail led up the hillside. While I suspected he intended we head that way, I still couldn't make out the final destination.

Eoghanan gathered me in his arms, kissing me down the side of my cheek until his lips landed tenderly on my own. "I love ye more than ye can ever know. I hope this trip hasna been too difficult for ye, Grace. I know ye are unaccustomed to traveling on horseback."

"It's been wonderful," I told him, meaning it. "I'm just using muscles I don't normally use, and they're screaming right now." I laughed. "I love an adventure, and you've certainly given me one." I'd lived nothing but one long adventure since the moment we met, and I couldn't help wondering if the rest of our lives together would seem the same to me.

"With my face resting against him, I breathed in his heady scent, undeniably male after so many days on the road. He smelled of sweat and earth and smoke from the fires we'd built at night. All combined, it was a comforting, surprisingly appealing smell, and I loved it.

"Ye are a wonder, wife—beautiful and strong and unafraid to try anything new. I am amazed by ye, and amazed and honored ye have chosen to have me by yer side through this life we've been given. I will spend it thanking ye for it in whatever way I can. I want to touch the part of yer soul that has been joined with mine.

"Eoghanan . . . " I sighed and lifted my head to look at him. "I don't think there's another man alive or dead that has ever spoken as beautifully to his wife as you do."

He kissed me, his beard tickling my nose. "In case ye haven't noticed, Grace, I am not a common man." He lifted a brow, his eyes twinkling. "'Tis, perhaps, the poet in me that makes me so."

"Hicumm...." The deep noise came from behind, and I twisted to find a man in his mid to late forties standing with his arms crossed and a pleased expression in his eyes. "If ye be a poet, then I am laird of yer brother's castle. Now, introduce me to yer new bride."

Eoghanan stepped away to greet the man but kept one hand on the small of my back, nudging me along with him. "'Tis good to see ye, Tinley. This is my wife, Grace."

I smiled and nodded to him, trying my best not to say much and inspire the usual questions about my strange accent.

"Do ye have it ready for us?" Eoghanan went for the horse, bringing it up alongside us.

"Aye, my wife helped in the preparations. I think ye will find it to yer liking. Doona ye worry about yer beast. I shall take good care of him until ye are ready to return home. There's enough food to last ye a week if ye need it, though I expect the lass will grow tired of ye far sooner than that."

Talk of preparations only heightened my curiosity further. Eoghanan must have sent a rider ahead of us to request from Tinley whatever awaited us.

Eoghanan handed the reins over to the man then reached for my hand. "I have no doubt that ye are right, but I'll do my best to keep her as long as I can."

"Aye, I'm sure ye shall. She is far too pretty for ye, even before what happened to yer face."

The man's words made me flinch. I'd never known Eoghanan without the scars, which made it easy to forget that once his face and body had been entirely undamaged by Niall's blade. He looked perfect to me now. The realization that others saw him as injured, different from how he once was, didn't set well with me.

No matter what I thought of the man's words, Eoghanan seemed unbothered by them, only nodding in the man's direction as he pulled me toward the winding trail.

"Aye, she is. Thank ye for everything." He pointed to one of the packs hanging off the horse. "Ye'll find yer payment in there."

I waited to speak until Tinley was out of sight, making sure to look down at my feet as I climbed so I wouldn't step on the bottom of my dress. "If you'd warned me, I could have packed my jeans."

Eoghanan chuckled, continuing his trek upward. "No, ye wouldna have. The first time I saw ye in such things I couldna look away. I willna have another man see ye dressed such."

I paused for a moment to hike up the dress. "Are there people who might see me wherever we are going? I assumed you'd be taking me somewhere a little more secluded."

"Aye, 'tis secluded. I doona wish to see anyone but ye for many days still."

We marched upward for the good part of an hour before I heard it—the loud rush of water so strong that I couldn't believe I hadn't noticed the sound before. The trail must have wound up the cliffside more than I'd thought, otherwise I couldn't imagine how the sound could have remained so well hidden. "Are we going to a waterfall? Is there a cabin near it that we are staying in or something?"

He slowed for the first time since we'd begun and smiled back at me in a way that told me I'd still not quite figured out his surprise. "No cabin."

"A castle, then? What? A river boat?"

His eyebrows pulled in. "A river boat? No, lass. Why doona ye just wait and see?"

"Patience was never my strong suit."

"Aye, I can see that. But 'tis mine, so no matter how many questions ye ask, I willna say a word. There is no need for ye to ask anything else, for we are there. But first..."

He moved to stand behind me, cupping both hands over my eyes.

"I'll trip if you make me walk with my eyes covered. My arms are too full of my dress for me to even catch myself."

"I'll catch ye, just step forward and turn when I tell ye to."

He didn't remove his hands from my face until I could feel the spray of the water against my skin. "Now, ye may look."

cMillan Castle

Bebop was sleeping, but Cooper could still see that his grandfather was worried. He could tell by the deep lines in his forehead and his wrinkled brow. Cooper knew how he felt. For some reason, he was worried, too.

He approached the chair where Bebop slept quietly, hoping he wouldn't wake him up as he crawled carefully into his lap. He should've known better though. Bebop was always a light sleeper, and his light blue eyes flew open as soon as Cooper settled onto his lap.

"What? Oh good, it's you, Coop. What's my favorite grandson up to? I was just resting my eyes for a while."

Cooper smiled, reaching up to try and stuff the puff of white hair that stuck out the side of his ear back inside. "I'm your *only* grandson, Bebop. And you can't fool me. I know what it means when you say you're resting your eyes—it means that you're sleeping."

Bebop reached up to swat his hand away. "Sleeping? No, I don't sleep during the day."

Cooper didn't argue but nodded to let Bebop know that he knew he did.

"And just because you're my only grandson doesn't mean that you can't be my favorite. What did you and your father do this morning?"

Cooper shifted on Bebop's lap so that he could face him. "We rode with Ba-o into the village and helped him pick up a crib for the baby that's coming. It's really pretty, Bebop. He had some man who can do super cool things with a block of wood make it."

"I should like to see it. Were you a big help?"

Cooper shrugged. He knew he was still too small to be much help to anybody. "I tried, but not really. Hey, can I ask you something, Bebop? What's bothering you so much?"

"What do you mean, son? Nothing's bothering me."

Cooper shook his head. He knew grown-ups sometimes lied to him to protect him, but he didn't like it. "That's not true, Bebop. I've known you my whole life, and I know that you're worried. Now, what's it about?"

Cooper knew the moment Bebop would tell him, because his grandfather reached up to mess with his hair, chuckling slightly as he always did when Cooper surprised him.

"I'll tell you, if I'd been as smart as you are when I was a child, I would have gotten in so much less trouble." Bebop paused. "Or maybe more, hard to tell, really. Would you believe me if I told you that you're right when you say I'm worried, but what worries me the most is I don't know why? Just a feeling...like something's coming that I'm powerless to stop. Do you understand that?"

It was like Bebop took the words right out of his head. Cooper nodded and leaned into him. "I do understand. Do you want to know why?"

Bebop reached his arm around him to hug him tight. "Why?"

"Because I feel the same way, Bebop, and I don't know why."

Brendon Falls

As promised, there was no cabin, castle, or riverboat when I opened my eyes. Instead, I stood perilously close to the edge of the cliff, my feet on a small foot-worn trail that led behind the waterfall. I couldn't see how anybody could make it behind the powerful rush of water without being swept into it.

"It's beautiful."

Eoghanan slid his hands from my eyes, moved them down my arms, and gathered them around me, pulling me close. "Aye, and so is what lies behind it."

"Behind it?" Even if we could manage to follow the trail, it would have been impossible for Tinley or anyone else to carry supplies and whatever else they'd left us along that path.

"Aye." He bent his head down next to mine while I looked nervously at the narrow, rocky trail.

"Well, you go right ahead, mister, because I'm not doing it."

"Do heights frighten ye, Grace?"

"I would be an utter fool if that drop didn't frighten me. Only an idiot would try to walk behind that rushing water." I leaned into him so he would take a step back. I felt like a huge disappointment after Eoghanan's beautiful speech to me about how I was always up for an adventure, but although the view was beautiful, I found myself ready to step away from the ledge.

"Aye, ye are verra right, lass. I wouldna allow ye to get inside the cave by way of the trail even if ye wished it. Do ye not remember when ye fell in my bedchamber at the inn? If ye canna walk across a room without meeting the floor, I doona wish to see ye try to manage that."

I stepped back, pushing us both farther from the ledge. "I

remember it very well, but I didn't just fall. I was startled by your scream because you'd singed your hand with hot water from the faucet."

"I told ye, lass, that I don't scream."

"Yeah, right. Whatever." I smirked at him. "I know a scream when I hear one."

He smiled wide, as if the memory brought him great joy, despite his embarrassment. I was sure it did; it certainly did me. It was the first day any real flirtation had begun between us.

"So, there's a cave behind this, huh?" I asked. "And just how do we get back there?"

He stepped away and took my hand, winking back at me over his shoulder. "This way."

We walked up a rocky staircase that I'd not noticed earlier. At the top, the steps turned downward, leading underneath the river feeding the waterfall. I found the engineering of it amazing, albeit utterly baffling. Without the use of modern tools, it seemed impossible that such a place could exist. "Who did this? It's truly astonishing."

He paused a few steps in front of me, answering over his shoulder. "No one knows. Not many know of its existence now. 'Tis truly a place of magic."

I didn't doubt it. As we stepped into the cave itself, I couldn't come up with any other explanation for the dwelling other than the use of magic from another like Morna. "Men didn't create this."

It wasn't a question, and he understood my meaning. "I doona think so, either. 'Twas a question I meant to ask Morna. If she knew of the witch who created this place."

"Perhaps it was Morna." I moved about the room, entirely awestruck by its beauty. The magic in the room was palpable.

Candles flickered from every corner of the stone space, highlighting the surprisingly large, round feather bed that sat against the back wall. It was draped in thick coverings. Looking at the warm, lush bed made me realize that I wasn't cold. That in and of itself was enough to convince me of the magic that lingered in the room.

"This is...Eoghanan, I hardly know what to say."

He smiled, leaning a hand against the wall opposite me. "Touch the stones, Grace. 'Tis the only way we could stay so close to the spray and remain warm."

They were warm, almost hot to the touch, and I closed my eyes at the pleasant sensation. "Oh, that's wonderful. I was just wondering at it, actually. I wondered how it was that I wasn't freezing in here, so close to the spray of the water."

A warm breath traveled down my neck, and I opened my eyes to find Eoghanan standing over me, his deep green eyes staring into mine. "Are ye hungry, lass?"

My stomach growled, as if on cue, and I laughed into his neck. "Very."

e were both famished after days on the road and dined happily on an assortment of bread, ale, and meat pies made for us by Tinley's wife—all of it delicious. By the time we'd had our fill, the sun began to dip down into the sky, casting a spectacle of light through the water and into the cave.

I stood from the small table where the food had been so beautifully laid out and ventured nearer the room's edge, hesitantly extending a hand into the running water. Its force sent my arm back down to my side, but I pulled it upward once again, enjoying the feeling of the water's power running through my fingers, its spray splashing onto my face and body, getting my dress rather wet.

"I think it best ye step back before ye soak yerself through to the bone."

I laughed but stepped away. Eoghanan grabbed me in an instant then lifted me in the air, swinging me over his shoulder as he stepped into the spray, drenching us both in the cool water.

I gasped and floundered against him, my laughter drowned out by the water that covered us. Once we were both dripping wet, he stepped back, setting me on my feet while he laughed deeply enough for the noise to reverberate off the stone.

"What did you do that for? I thought you didn't like water—especially the sound of it falling." I pulled all my hair around over one shoulder, ringing out some of the water.

"I doona like water, but this is a special place, and 'tis too beautiful to dislike." His eyes skimmed over my body where my wet clothing clung to every curve. "Do ye know how breathtaking ye are, Grace?"

Despite the cold, heavy dress now glued to my body, I warmed through instantly, blushing as I combed my blonde hair through with my fingers. "Not so breathtaking really, I imagine. You're just partial. You have to say things like that now that I'm your wife."

He crossed his arms and shook his head, his own red hair dripping and shaggy once more. It grew quickly. Already he was in need of another cut.

"No, Grace. I doona have to say any such thing to ye. I know plenty of lads who doona think their wives to be pretty and wouldna tell them so just because they were married."

I frowned reactively. "Well, that's quite sad."

"'Tis verra true. I wouldna say it to ye if I dinna mean it, lass. I can scarcely breathe when I stand in front of ye, even dripping like a wet dog as ye are now."

"The wet dog look is your doing. I was content to let the water touch my hands."

"Aye, 'tis. Now, turn around and let me help ye out of yer dress so we may let it dry."

The laces were difficult to maneuver now that they were wet, but Eoghanan managed them nicely.

Soon, with our wet clothes off and cast aside, I crawled into the bed. "I could stay here forever with ye, Grace, behind this waterfall in our own little world." Eoghanan's voice was husky, his eyes hazy with love for me as he moved across the room to join me. He ducked his head as he crawled into the bed with me. I had never imagined until now that I could love a man so completely. It frightened me, the sense of complete connection, simple understanding, and unwavering commitment we had for each other. As he held onto the side of my face, brushing his thumb over my cheek as he always did to comfort me, I knew that it frightened him, too. The love and joy that rose within me paled in comparison to any experience I'd ever imagined having with a partner.

In his eyes, I could see what I meant to him—the love, adoration, and respect he held for me. Unwillingly, it brought tears to my eyes and quickly he kissed them away.

We kissed, and as we did so, I imagined us to be much like the water in the river above the waterfall, the unexplainable feeling of exhilaration and terror reaching an immeasurable level as we neared the point of falling, of rolling off the cliff's edge.

Our breathing escalated such that it was all I could hear, the sound of the rushing water muted by the noise of our ragged breathing. The kiss ended, and from somewhere beneath the heart-pounding fog, Eoghanan's voice called out to me, pleading with me to open my eyes.

"Look at me, Grace."

As I opened my eyes and looked into his, my past was swept away like a leaf in the river. What I saw in its place was a future more beautiful than the waterfall or this room. A future of good times, and hard times, of happiness and tears. A future we would build and get through together, hand-in-hand. And I was ready for whatever it brought because I knew that I could do anything with this man by my side. I had found my strength, my heart—all the best parts of myself—within the soul of another who was now my husband.

CHAPTER 41

*M*cMillan Castle

The slip of the poison into the man's drinking water had been far too easy to accomplish. Jinty knew it would settle into his stomach overnight. She'd at least hoped for a challenge, but the end result would be the same. The boy's father would fall ill and lose consciousness for most of the day, allowing her plenty of time to take the lad away before Eoghanan and his new wife returned this evening.

Jinty sat back from her place amongst the trees to watch the sun rise. The boy and his father would do what they did every day after their morning meal—come to sit by the pond. Only this time, they wouldn't be alone. She would be waiting for the poison to do its work.

hatever had worried him and Bebop over the last few days was coming for them today. Cooper didn't know why or what would happen, but he knew it just as sure as he knew he'd love dinosaurs every day of his whole life. There was no other reason why he would have dreamed of the stone.

Everybody thought he couldn't keep secrets, but it was one of the things Cooper was best at. He'd not told Mom that E-o could travel through time or that Morna was a witch when he'd promised he wouldn't. He'd not told Mom about the time Dad lost him at the city park after he promised Dad he wouldn't. And he'd not told anyone about the story Morna had told him and the promise she'd made him the day he'd thrown the black stone into the pond.

He could remember everything she'd said when she'd pulled him aside during their tour of the castle.

"Cooper," she'd said to him. "I know that ye took my traveling stones and what ye mean to do with them. Ye are a fine lad, and I trust ye to make the decision ye believe ye must, but I need ye to remember something verra important. Can ye do that for me?"

He loved when grown-ups entrusted him with important tasks. He'd nodded as he answered her. "I'll remember. I don't forget anything."

"I believe that, lad. Now, this red one here, keep it tucked safely in yer jeans if ye decide to throw the black ones. Yer parents will do all they can to keep ye safe, but sometimes there are things in this world from which no one can protect us. But, ye are luckier than most, lad, for ye have a verra kind and powerful witch watching over ye."

He'd laughed then. He knew that Morna spoke of herself.

"I'll be watching from afar, but I canna keep eyes on ye every moment. Should ye need me, throw this rock into the pond, and I'll come for ye. I have not returned to my own time since I left it, but for ye, child, I'll come running."

That talk had been weeks ago, but the morning after his dream, right after breakfast he went straight to where he'd last left the rock, his worry still weighing heavily on his little mind. He pulled apart the plastic shell of one of his dinosaur eggs, glancing down at the rock inside. Lifting the shiny red stone out of its home, he tucked it away just as Dad called to him from the hallway so they could spend some time at the pond.

Despite all his baby teeth that remained, Cooper had a strong feeling that after today no one would be able to call him a baby. Something bad was coming to the castle. But if he could remember to throw the stone at just the right time, perhaps he could be a hero.

***

Our honeymoon continued in a blur of lazy days spent with food, ale, and romance. By the time our clothes had fully dried several days later, we were both ready to return home to Cooper.

I'd never been away from him for so long, and each hoof step that remained until I held him in my arms was one hoof step too many.

"What time do you think we will make it back to the castle?"

Eoghanan had sensed my desire to hurry much earlier, and he'd picked up our pace hours ago.

"This morning I would have told ye nightfall, but we have ridden well throughout the day. I am pleased to tell ye that we approach McMillan territory as we speak, lass."

I looked out over the vast land, the village off to the left, the castle still miles ahead of us. It was a relief to know that I neared my son, and I relaxed a little until smoke billowing up from trees separated from the village caught my attention. There was nothing ominous about the sight, but an inexplicable desire to turn our horse in the direction of the smoke filled me.

"Eoghanan." I pointed. "What do you suppose that is over there?"

It took him a moment to respond, and I turned to look up at him.

"I doona know for sure, lass. I know it seems odd, but I have not noticed such a place before. It must be a cottage."

"Could it be . . . ?" I didn't want to finish my question, but it was where my mind went immediately. The witch, Jinty, lived on McMillan territory—Eoghanan had said Baodan had raided her cottage. But surely a witch who knew others were looking for her wouldn't be stupid enough to light a fire that would signal she'd returned home. If the smoke did, indeed, come from Jinty's cottage, something was very wrong.

"Jinty." Eoghanan's conclusion came just a few seconds after my own, and his arms grew tense around me as he urged the horse forward more quickly.

He was now as eager as I to reach the castle.

Cooper knew his dad could be easily distracted, so when Bebop caught them in the hall on their way out to the pond and started chatting away, Cooper simply smiled, skipping off in the direction of the water alone.

The rock bounced up and down in his pocket, but he kept his hand cupped over it, protecting the magic stone that he knew he would have to use today. He could feel it—the danger coming toward the castle.

Someone meant to harm him. He'd seen the shadow approaching him for nights while he slept—the same scary dream that left him with plenty to think about each morning. He was frightened, but he had to be brave. Bravery was all that would protect him until he sent for Morna, and he knew that even after he threw the rock he would be alone for a time—the travel wasn't always instant.

Cooper rounded the curve that led to the back side of the pond and stopped still. He saw her watching him among the trees, the same lady E-o had forced to leave the castle on one of the nights of the gathering. She couldn't see him looking at her, and he knew that was best. It gave him a moment to think, to gather his courage and slip the rock from his pocket.

Mom never let him watch scary movies, but Dad sometimes did because he knew that Cooper was brave enough to know they weren't real. But now, as he watched the woman hiding among the trees, he felt like he was in the middle of his very own scary movie. If he wanted to live, he had to be smarter than all the people who ended up dead in those movies. He couldn't make her angry, and he needed to keep her talking.

Cooper knew she'd grab him just as soon as he got close enough to her, so he took his time walking along the pond's edge. Once he stood in front of her, he turned his back so that he faced away from her. It took only a moment before the trees rustled behind him, and he knew she would reach for him.

As her hands clasped around his mouth, he threw the rock into the water, allowing the stranger to take him away.

he woman's cottage was only a short ride from the castle. For the whole ride, Cooper sat with his eyes closed, praying that Morna would arrive soon. When nothing happened after the woman yanked him off the horse and dragged him inside, Cooper knew he would have to keep her busy for a time—to keep her from harming him right away.

Cooper swallowed hard, hoping his voice wouldn't shake as he talked. No matter how afraid he truly was, he didn't want his captor to know that. "Wow, this is some place you have here, lady. What's your name?"

To his surprise, she answered him with no hint of anger in her voice. For some reason, that frightened him more than it would have had she responded angrily. He realized she didn't want him scared because he would be more difficult to kill—like the time he'd joined Bebop on a deer hunting excursion—you couldn't scare the animals, or they'd run.

"I'm Jinty. And what is yer name, lad?"

"Cooper."

Jinty nodded at him and pointed at a chair along the back wall.

Understanding, Cooper moved to sit as he grabbed onto the cup she extended toward him. The smell was enough to make him pull up his nose in disgust. He knew in that instant that he couldn't drink whatever was inside.

"Drink up, lad. I know that I frightened ye. I dinna mean to. My quarrel is not with ye. I doona wish to make it harder on ye than it needs to be."

He shook his head, handing it back to her. "No thank you, ma'am. I'm not real thirsty."

She pushed it back to him. "I dinna ask ye if ye were thirsty."

Cooper held the cup cautiously, looking down at the thick brown liquid that smelled like the inside of his cousin Harry's diaper. How dumb did Jinty think he was? Had she never seen *Snow White?* The thought tickled him, and he accidentally laughed out loud for a brief moment. Of course she hadn't seen it—there were no movies here.

"I doona know why ye are laughing, lad, but ye best cease this instant. Now, drink."

Cooper knew he had to think of something fast. If he really drank it, he would die. He just needed to make her think he had gulped it down. He had to fool her until Morna could get here.

"Do you have any sugar?" he asked hesitantly, worried she would get angry.

"Sugar? No, doona say another word to me until ye drink it, or I shall force it down yer throat."

Cooper swallowed hard, pushing away his fear. "I only wanted something to make it taste better so it will be easier to drink."

Jinty's eyebrows pulled together. "Not a thing will make it sweeter, lad."

A sudden noise rapped against the window, and Cooper saw his opportunity. As Jinty jerked her head in the direction of the sound, Cooper quickly dripped some of the liquid onto the floor. Unfortunately, he didn't take into account that she would see the spill once she turned back to him.

All of Jinty's restrained anger released itself the instant she saw what he'd done, and he didn't have the chance to stand and run before she stood before him and gripped his face, forcing his mouth open as she poured the sticky liquid inside.

Cooper screamed and choked, but a flash of movement in the window behind her caught his eyes. Within the next moment, the door to the cabin flew open to reveal Morna.

With the flick of Morna's wrists, the cup Jinty held against his mouth flew out of her hands and up against her face, crushing her nose as she fell to the ground, unconscious.

Cooper slid from the chair and ran toward Morna, throwing his arms around her legs. "I knew you would come, but I'm afraid you're too late. She made me drink it." Cooper sank down on the floor, suddenly feeling sleepy. He'd never expected to die this way —he'd always hoped he'd get to meet his end in a real-life *Jurassic Park*. "I'm guessing I'll die soon."

The laughter that erupted from Morna hurt his feelings. He had always thought she liked him.

"Ach, lad. Do ye really think I'd let her kill ye? I saw her lifting the cup to yer lips, and I spelled it into prune juice. Other than a loose stool or two, I think ye shall survive."

Cooper exhaled a breath he hadn't known he held. "What? Are you telling me the truth?"

"Of course I am. Now, stand yerself up. We need to secure the beastly witch before she wakes up."

Cooper looked down at Jinty as he stood, wrinkling up his nose in disgust at the blood that was running down her face.

"What are you going to do with her?"

"Do ye want me to tell ye the truth, Cooper? Or do ye wish me to tell ye what I should tell a child?"

Cooper turned his head at her—of course she already knew his answer. "The truth...always."

"Aye, fine. I'll kill her, lad. Once she wakes and we've had a bit of a discussion, I will put her in the ground. No one harms my family, lad. Does that bother you?"

Cooper didn't know what to think about that. It was wrong to kill people, but this woman had also meant to kill him. "Has she hurt other people?"

Morna nodded. "Many. She was nearly responsible for Eoghanan's death, and she would have killed ye too if ye hadna thrown the wee rock."

"E-o!" Cooper shook his head in disbelief. He liked E-o too much to imagine him dead. "Okay, do it, Morna. I don't want her to hurt anyone else. But..." he hesitated. He didn't wish for Morna to think him weak. "Don't hurt her. I don't think there's really any need for that."

Morna's face dropped in disappointment, but she nodded as she pointed outside the door of the cottage. "Aye, fine. Once she is awake, I willna cause her much pain, but now that she is asleep, I willna bring her back around carefully."

Cooper watched with wide eyes as Morna mumbled a spell underneath her breath and turned to leave the cottage. With each step, Jinty's body dragged along behind Morna on its own, the blood from her nose leaving a nasty trail.

CHAPTER 43

The sight of Jeffrey collapsed next to a pool of his own blood and vomit brought me to my knees. Finding one of Cooper's shoes next to him sent me into hysterics. I could do nothing but scream and cry over Jeffrey's limp body as Eoghanan checked to see if he lived. His pulse was strong and steady, which served as some small relief, though it did nothing to numb my panic over Cooper's absence.

It took only moments before my screams sent Baodan, Mitsy, and Charles running toward us from the castle. Within seconds of their taking in the scene, I was gathered up in Mitsy's arms as she tried to calm me.

"This poison is the same that was used on me the night of Osla's death, the same that our mother consumed for so long."

Eoghanan's voice was strong, but I could hear the panic and worry in it. Not to mention the guilt he already felt at not disposing of the witch before now.

"'Tis Jinty that provided Niall the poison. The witch," Eoghanan explained. "I believe we passed her cottage on the way here."

"Aye." Baodan spoke next to him, reaching out to steady

Charles who'd paled significantly. "Ye and Grace ride in the direction ye believe her to be at once, and I will send men after ye immediately. I will stay to aid in Jeffrey's recovery." He looked quickly to Charles and then to me. "He will recover. The poison in this dose is not meant to kill him."

I knew I would hyperventilate if I didn't get a grip on my panic. The over-rush of emotions would dull my senses, and I needed my wits about me in order to save Cooper. Grabbing onto Mitsy's hand, I pulled myself up and turned to mount our horse, saying nothing to Eoghanan who had already turned in the same direction.

He lifted me quickly onto the back of the horse, speaking calmly to me as he mounted behind me. "She willna have hurt him, Grace. Not yet. Not without someone to witness it; without that, the act would be pointless, for none would know for certain if 'twas her. I promise ye, I will die before I let her hurt him or ye."

I breathed in deeply, boxing up any emotion that wouldn't serve to help me save my son. The witch was a fool if she thought she would end the day any place other than six feet under.

A sharp groan from behind me caused me to turn my head, and I looked to see Mitsy leaning forward, one hand on her back.

She saw me staring and waved us onward, smiling through the pain. "Go on. Get out of here, the both of you. It's just...gas."

Eoghanan nodded and nudged the horse into a run, but not before I heard her scream once more.

"Holy crap, Baodan, my water broke."

I did nothing but pray for my son's safety as we galloped toward the pillar of smoke we'd seen earlier. It took us mere minutes to reach it, but it felt like days. I flung myself from the horse's back the instant Eoghanan pulled the beast to a stop, only pausing at the sound of Eoghanan's urgent voice behind me.

"Grace, no!"

His voice was as panicked and raspy as I'd ever heard it. Only when his arms came around me to restrain me from stepping toward the cottage did I see what he looked at.

A trail of thick, fresh blood ran down the steps of the cottage, marking a trail all the way to the back of it.

"No! Oh, God, no!" Sobs racked my body as I collapsed in his arms, screaming uncontrollably.

"Grace." Eoghanan shook my shoulders roughly. "Grace, shut yer mouth. This is not over, yet. The witch is still here. Now if ye canna stop yer screaming until we find her, I shall gag ye and strap ye to the horse."

The calmness of his voice shocked me into silence. How could he not be as lost in the thralls of grief as I was? I looked up into his eyes, ready to throttle him for not sharing my pain, when I understood.

His grief had been temporarily pushed aside by his rage. He would kill the witch for what she had done.

I said nothing, only choked back my tears for the second time and followed him around the cottage where he was forced to clamp his hands over my mouth once again to keep me from crying out in relief.

There, standing not fifty yards from us, was Cooper, his hands on both hips as he looked in the direction of the billowing smoke and the woman who stood in front of it—Morna.

It was only then, after my eyes adjusted to the shock of seeing Morna in such an unexpected place, that my ears began to hear what she said to Jinty, who she had strapped up against a tree. I recognized panic in the young woman's eyes.

"If yer only transgression was being foolish enough to fall for Niall's lies, I suppose ye could be forgiven, but ye are responsible for the deaths of others. No only that, but ye tried to harm my family. No one does that, lass."

The witch snarled, thrashing against the magic chains that held her, as she spit at Morna.

I threw a quick glance to Cooper, who had yet to see us. I expected him to look afraid; instead, he looked fascinated. I wanted to run toward him but refrained, not wishing to interrupt the witch's confrontation.

"Ye can twist yerself about in these chains all day, curse me under yer breath all ye wish, but I am more powerful than ye will ever be, lass. Ye will die today, but take comfort that ye willna suffer. Ye can thank the boy for that. I will snap yer neck with the flick of my wrist before I toss ye into the flames."

"Do it." Jinty's words were raspy and hideous, the hatred in her eyes enough to chill me through. "But with my last breath, I curse ye and all yer..."

She was given no chance to finish. Before her last words, there was a terrible crack, and the witch's head fell limp against her shoulder. The chains that held her body vanished, and she fell back into the flames, disappearing before our eyes.

Morna turned away from the fire and walked toward Cooper. She spoke to him gently. "Are ye all right, lad? I dinna mean to scare ye, but the lass was mad if she thought I'd let her curse my family at the end."

Cooper nodded, giving her a brief grin before his eyes finally shifted in our direction. As he ran toward me, Morna turned and addressed Eoghanan as if she'd known we'd been there all along.

"Eoghanan, for God's sake, release Grace. Jinty is gone now. Ye doona mean to keep her from hugging her son, do ye?"

"How are ye here, Morna?"

"Ach." Morna waved a dismissing hand toward the pillar of smoke. "Cooper sent for me."

Eoghanan released me, and I charged Cooper. He wrapped his arms around me but pulled away as I clung to him. "What's the matter with you, Mom? Did you not have a good time on your honeymoon?"

"What? Cooper, are you joking? You were just kidnapped, and you think I'm upset because I didn't have a good time on my honeymoon?"

"But, Mom..." He pulled back as far as he could in my vice-like hold on him. "I wasn't kidnapped. Not but for a minute, and I knew Morna was coming for me, anyway, so I just didn't worry too much."

"You didn't worry." The tone of my voice seemed to be frightening him more than anything else had so I struggled to pull it into one of some normalcy. "Cooper, you worry about everything."

"I didn't because of the red rock, Mom." He said it so plainly, as if I were the fool for not knowing what he meant.

Morna spoke as she waved us all near to her. "Shall we return the three of ye to McMillan Castle? And Cooper," she reached out to pat his shoulder, "I think it might be best if ye allow me to explain."

CHAPTER 44

hether it was really Cooper's red rock that had summoned Morna, or just simply her uncanny ability to know everything that went on with her family, no one knew. And no one cared. We all realized how unusual it was for her to make a travel herself—having not done so since she'd left her own time as a young girl.

She'd not only arrived in time to save Cooper, but to provide a remedy for Jeffrey, and to gift Mitsy with a somewhat more pleasant birthing experience. After the chaotic and emotionally-draining afternoon, all was returned to right within the castle by evening.

Mitsy and Baodan welcomed their beautiful and ridiculously chunky baby boy, Rodric McMillan, at sundown. For the first time in his life, Cooper was out for the count before supper. His little adventure with the horrific witch, Jinty, had been far more traumatic on his parents and stepfather than it had been on him.

I sat on the edge of Cooper and Jeffrey's bed watching them both sleep when Eoghanan appeared in the doorway, his hand extended toward me.

"Come to bed, lass. I doona think either of them shall open an eye until morning."

I stood. After kissing Cooper on the forehead, I joined Eoghanan, taking his hand as we walked to our bedchamber. When we reached the doorway, I turned to stop him, gathering his face in my hands as I kissed him gently.

"My entire life, there have been only two men that I loved so much I couldn't measure it, couldn't get a grasp on how much they meant to me, couldn't fathom what my life would look like without them in it. Now...there are three. You are the person I didn't even know I wanted, but needed so desperately. One day, I want to make two dozen more Coopers with you."

He ran his thumb along my brow, kissing me gently on the top of my head as he gathered me in his arms and carried me inside. "I want nothing more than that, Grace. But, lass, mayhap we doona start tonight."

I laughed as he lay me on top of the bed, and nodded in agreement as we crawled beneath the covers in unison. For the first time in a week, we lay in each other's arms and slept like rocks.

The night defined 'perfection.'

wo Weeks Later

Cooper walked hand-in-hand with Morna to the pond's edge, his heart a little heavy at the thought of saying goodbye.

"Are you sure you have to leave? There's a bunch of rooms in this castle, and most of them are empty. Believe me, I know. I'm always sneaking inside them."

Morna squeezed his hand before bending to hug him. "Aye, Jerry needs me much more than all of ye. He canna cook to save his life. I worry he'll starve to death without me."

Cooper laughed, pulling one of the black stones out of his pocket and extending it in Morna's direction. "I guess you're right. Are you sure you want to go back this way? You get kinda wet."

"I think it only fair that I subject myself to the same treatment I did each of ye, aye?"

Cooper hugged Morna's neck before pulling away. "Yeah, I

guess so, but I hope you're a good swimmer. Hey, can I ask you one more question before you leave?"

"Aye, what do ye wish to ask?"

"It's about my dad. He's so alone here. Everybody has someone else but him."

Cooper watched as Morna stood and smiled down at him, twirling the black stone through her fingers. "Ye are here for him."

He shook his head, exasperated. "I don't count. He needs somebody to kiss and stuff...like Mom and E-o."

Morna winked at him before she drew her arm back to let loose the stone, her words barely escaping her lips before the rock touched the water, and she vanished.

"All in due time, wee Cooper. All in due time."

Turn the page for a sneak peek of *Jeffrey's Only Wish*.

CHAPTER 1

Mitchell Family Estate—Lake Placid, New York—Present Day

I'm not saying I didn't question my sanity the moment I'd relented to Grace's request that I take a trip with Cooper to the present to visit his grandparents without her.

Still, I told myself repeatedly that I was doing this for Cooper —that he needed it, that it was important for my son to know his grandparents, to see his aunts who were up in arms about our long absence. All of that was true, but what's the saying...*from the mouths of babes?* It's too true. So many children are too smart for their own good, but my kid really does top them all. The squirt was going on twenty as a toddler and is now six-going-on-forty.

Cooper knew it was more than my willingness to do anything for him that brought us here, but it wasn't until he told me so outright that I realized just how thoroughly I'd been lying to myself.

We'd just turned onto the mile long, tree-lined driveway leading up to the Mitchell family estate when Cooper leaned forward from his seat in the back and rubbed the side of my arm sympathetically.

"Dad, you must really hate it at the castle."

"What?" His words caught me off-guard. No matter my thoughts on its lack of running water and the questionable hygiene of ninety-eight percent of the population, I'd never complained to anyone about my life in the seventeenth century. Why would I? I had nothing to complain about. I knew how lucky I was to be living such an unbelievably extraordinary life. And I was happy there, but that didn't mean I wasn't also ready to feel like a normal guy for a day or two.

After arriving in the past, I quickly learned that no amount of time there would turn me into a man like Eoghanan and his clansmen. I couldn't ride a horse all day long without my backside getting sore, and I still couldn't chunk half a tree twenty yards or drink whiskey like it was water and stay standing for very long. Worst of all, I hated kilts—the essential clothing staple among all seventeenth century Scots. They were heavy and cumbersome, and there was something about not having separate leg holes that made me uneasy. No one was going to convince me to go commando in a kilt while riding, either.

Months of living in the past hadn't changed me from being the modern man I was. Despite the fact that men of that time, or at least the ones I knew, seemed to take quite well to women from modern times, the same could not be said for seventeenth century women. They did not take to me very well at all.

"Dad...hello...?"

"What?" I shook my head, my thoughts returning to Cooper. "I don't hate it. I was just ready for a break. I thought it would be a good opportunity to take a hot shower and maybe watch a football game."

"Dad." The tone of his voice made it clear that he didn't believe a word I'd said. "You're taking me to Grandfather's. He really doesn't like you."

"He used to." I frowned involuntarily. I really didn't like the old bag either, but I wished that Cooper hadn't been able to pick up on that.

"Yeah, he used to, but then you and Mom ran away from your wedding *and* you quit your job."

"Well, it doesn't really matter what he thinks about me, Coop. You know that he loves you, right?"

I could see my son nodding in the rearview mirror, although his face seemed less sure. "Yeah, he kinda does, but not like Bebop."

My father, Bebop as Cooper knew him, loved people more strongly than anyone I'd ever known in my life. "Grandfather couldn't love anybody the way Bebop does."

"Yep. Hey, so Dad, why'd you make me sit in the backseat? Mom's not here."

Once...only once, I'd allowed him to sit in the front seat when Grace wasn't around, and the chewing out she'd given me afterward had cured me of any such thoughts of ever letting it happen again.

"It doesn't matter that your mom's not here. It's not safe for you to sit up here yet."

My son was not the sort of boy to pout, not over something as trivial as sitting in the front seat, so when he slumped back and let out a long sigh, I knew what bothered him.

"Cooper, you know Morna would never ignore you. If she hasn't responded yet, there's a good reason."

Morna, our friendly witch and the one responsible for hurdling us through time, was Cooper's confidant and fellow schemer. Although Morna resided in the present, her magical abilities allowed them to be the strangest pair of cross-century pen pals.

"Yeah, but Dad, it's been four weeks, and she wasn't at her house when we went by. She would have known we were coming. Why wasn't she there? I'm worried about her, Dad."

Cooper didn't need to worry about Morna. By my calculations, the old broad should've been in the ground decades ago, and she was still going strong and no doubt would for some time to come.

"Coop, if I had to guess, she was probably just out tending to the sheep. Don't worry about it. She will respond to you, I'm certain. I have to ask you though—what was in this last letter? I usually help you write them, but this time you went to Bebop. Why?"

Whatever reason he had for keeping me out of the loop made me nervous. It meant he was busy scheming, and he knew he had my father wound so tight around his little finger he could make him an accomplice in anything.

"Oh, that." I could hear Cooper's smile in his voice. "I guess since I've already sent it and you can't do anything about it, I can tell you now."

"Son...what did you do?"

"Oh, you know, the same thing I've been tryin' to do for months now. I just asked her if she'd found you a lady yet."

Finding me a 'lady' had become Cooper's obsession from the moment Grace married Eoghanan.

"It's not Morna's job to find me a woman, Cooper. I can do that on my own."

Cooper said nothing, but made a noise of disagreement. I took his brief silence as an opportunity to change the subject.

"So, you remember that we can't tell anybody the truth about all of this, right?"

"Of course we can't. They'd think we're totally crazy." Cooper laughed, rising from his previously slumped state.

All Grace's family knew was that her business trip had been

extended indefinitely after she'd fallen in love, gotten married, and now, six months later, was pregnant. They also knew that my father and I had joined her and Cooper in Scotland, but that was the extent of their knowledge as to our new life. They would remain oblivious to the fact that we'd all decided to live happily ever after in the seventeenth century.

A sudden loud honk repeated itself as a red convertible came up on our tail, following so closely I reluctantly increased the car's speed.

"It's Aunt Jane!"

Cooper twisted so he could wave out the back window to her. She waved her arms at us frantically, taking her hands from the wheel. After she nearly veered into the trees, she gripped the wheel once again and Cooper faced the front, slightly embarrassed.

"I didn't mean to make her do that."

I waved a dismissive hand in his direction. "You didn't make her do anything. She's very good at driving horribly on her own."

Next to Grace, Jane was by far the most likeable Mitchell and really the only one who didn't walk on eggshells around Walter. I had immense respect for her. She was crass, funny, and friendly.

"Come on, Dad. Speed this rig up. I want to see Aunt Jane."

I pushed on the gas to keep Jane from ramming the back of us and scrunched my eyebrows in response to my son. "This rig? Where do you get this stuff?"

Cooper laughed, elated that he was about to be free to enjoy his favorite play toy—his Aunt Jane. "I don't know. It just comes to me, Dad."

We rounded the corner that revealed the Mitchell mansion, and reluctantly I placed the car in park. Unbuckling, Cooper flung the car door open and ran to the driver's side of Jane's car, waiting for her to open it to him. As she climbed out of the car, he threw his arms around her legs. "Aunt Jane. To the tree." He pointed down the path beside the house, leading to the extravagant tree house. "We gotta go before Grandfather comes out."

Jane laughed but stayed where she stood, shouting at me from beside her car. "Hey Jeffrey, I'd come say hello, but it sounds to me like this kid's got the right idea. I'll catch you later."

Shaking Cooper loose, she took off toward the path. "Race you, Coop. You better hurry." Turning as she ran, she yelled back to me, "Oh! And, I have some big news to share with all of you later."

I called after her, "That makes me nervous."

"Oh, it should." Her voice faded as she disappeared around the side of the house.

Squealing with laughter, Cooper took off after her, leaving me to unload the car alone. I exited the vehicle slowly, wanting to take as much time as I possibly could. When I faced the house, only one person waited for me in the driveway.

Cooper's grandfather—Walter.

Get *Jeffrey's Only Wish* to continue the series.

Jeffrey's Only Wish
(The Magical Matchmaker's Legacy - Book 4.5)

USA TODAY BESTSELLING AUTHOR
BETHANY CLAIRE
A Sweet, Scottish, Time-Travel Romance
JEFFREY'S ONLY WISH
A NOVELLA
The Magical Matchmaker's Legacy
BOOK 4.5

Dear Reader,

I hope you enjoyed *Morna's Accomplice (The Magical Matchmaker's Legacy - Book 4)*. I fell in love with little Cooper and loved writing Eoghanan's love story, as well. Please continue the series with *Jeffrey's Only Wish* where you will find what Cooper and Morna are up to.

As an author, I love feedback from readers. You are the reason that I write, and I love hearing from you. If you would like to connect, there are several ways you can do so. You can reach out to me on Facebook or on Twitter or visit my Pinterest boards. If you want to read excerpts from my books, listen to audiobook samples, learn more about me, and find some cool downloadable files related to the books, visit my website (www.bethanyclaire.com).

The best way to stay in touch is to subscribe to my newsletter. Go to my website and click the Mailing List link in the header. If you don't hear from me regularly, please check your spam folder or junk mail to make sure my messages aren't ending up there. Please set up your email to allow my messages through to you so you never miss a new book, a chance to win great prizes or a possible appearance in your area.

Finally, if you enjoyed this book, I would appreciate it so much if you would recommend it to your friends and family. And if you would please take time to review it on Goodreads and/or your favorite retailer site, it would be a great help. Reviews can be tough to come by these days, and you, the reader, have the power to make or break a book.

Thank you so much for reading. I hope you choose to journey with me through the other books in the series.

All my best,
Bethany

BETHANY CLAIRE is a USA Today bestselling author of swoon-worthy, Scottish romance and time travel novels. Bethany loves to immerse her readers in worlds filled with lush landscapes, hunky Scots, lots of magic, and happy endings.

She has two ornery fur-babies, plays the piano every day, and loves Disney and yoga pants more than any twenty-something really should. She is most creative after a good night's sleep and the perfect cup of tea. When not writing, Bethany travels as much as she possibly can, and she never leaves home without a good book to keep her company.

If you want to read more about Bethany or if you're curious about when her next book will come out, please visit her website at: www.bethanyclaire.com, where you can sign up to receive email notifications about new releases.

Connect with Bethany on social media or visit her website for lots of book extras:

www.bethanyclaire.com

ACKNOWLEDGMENTS

This book was one of my favorites to write, so it's been fun to discover this one again with the rewrites.

Thanks so much to J.J. Archer for the fabulous changes. Special thanks also to my proofreading team members who helped with this book: Karen Corboy, Elizabeth Halliday, Vivian Nwankpah, and Johnetta Ivey—you guys are awesome! And to Mom—I'll never be able to thank you enough.

www.ingramcontent.com/pod-product-compliance
Lightning Source LLC
Chambersburg PA
CBHW030019200726
48283CB00012B/687